THREE DEAD GODS

MORTALITY BITES SERIES

RAMY VANCE

KEEP EVOLVING STUDIOS

THREE DEAD GODS

PART I
A BEGINNING OF SORTS

Charon used to be the Ferryman of the Dead, guiding departed souls from the land of the living to whatever heaven or hell their worship condemned them to. But that was when the universe still had heavens and hells, when the world still had gods and souls that still needed ferrying.

So much has changed since then, and Charon no longer guides the dead. He is, however, still a ferryman (for even the gods' departure cannot change everything). But instead of helping lost souls find their final destination, he ferries living humans from the shores of a human settlement to the beach of a nearby island where the mortals engage in something called a "picnic."

His new occupation was not assigned to him, but something he stumbled upon.

For you see, when the gods left with their final message echoing in his head—*"Thank you for believing in us, but it's not enough. We're leaving. Good luck"*—Charon had just completed his latest ferry and was paddling downstream on the river Styx.

As soon as the gods' words ceased, the normally calm river unsettled as a strong current began pulling his boat toward a single portal in the middle. His ferry flew through the hole (with him still on board —thank the GoneGods for small miracles) where he found himself on a lake he would later learn was called Lake Kashawigamog.

And so this is where Charon—the psychophomb, the Ferryman of the Dead, the now mortal boatsman—found himself the day everything he knew was taken away. On Lake Kashawigamog, with its little island where the humans needed ferrying so that they could picnic.

↔

When Charon ferried the dead, his fee was two copper coins—one for each eye. So when he started his new enterprise, he charged the humans the same two copper coins he always had. Two pennies to be ferried to the island, which by his estimation was a fair price.

The humans seemed to agree, were pleased by his fee.

He continued with this price for many months, until one particularly chatty human pointed out that in the world of the living, two pennies were of little value. Now Charon's fee has grown a hundredfold ... to two dollars.

At first, he worried that such an inflated price would deter the humans from using his services. But his worries were ill-founded, for the humans still gladly paid his fee.

↔

This is Charon's new lot in life—in his *mortal* life—and the old ferryman has adapted to it admirably. He enjoys the dialogs he has with these living humans during their short voyages. They are so filled with joy at the prospect of a pleasant day spent, and many are curious about his past, asking questions about the heavens and hells, about the gods, about what life was like when immortal beings were still immortal.

The chit-chat he has with living humans is so much more pleasant than his conversations with the souls he once ferried. Those conversations overflowed with concern: *What is heaven like? Does hell hurt? Is it really forever?*

Then there were those souls of ill-repute, the ones of power and greed who had opted for a life of luxury and an eternity in Hell. They would always try to bribe or threaten the ferryman, insisting that he divert his path to another, more pleasant plane. Their incessant prattle would last until the moment that RE or Maalik or Leviathan, or whichever other gatekeeper of Hell, finally took them away.

And, lest he forget, Charon had ferried the cowardly souls who jumped overboard in an attempt to swim away or drown rather than go to Hell. Foolish souls; one could not swim the currents of River Hubur, Sarasvati River, River Malvam or the River Styx without a ferry such as Charon's. And as for drowning? A soul cannot die twice.

"Like herding cats," suggests one particularly conversational human whom Charon has grown to like quite a lot.

"I know not what you mean," Charon says, looking at the human who rides his ferry several times a day, every day. It is evident that this human cares little for picnicking. He carries a hunger for knowledge, and given the number of times he has ridden in Charon's ferry, this human's hunger will never be sated.

"You know—cats. They don't listen, they're in it for themselves, not really team players."

Charon considers this as he guides his ferry across the calm waters of the lake. Certainly, the Egyptian god Seth was a being filled with wrath, but even he was always willing to work with the other Egyptian gods. And as for Bastet ... well, Bastet was a difficult being who cared little for others. But then again, so many gods were like that, and Charon cannot say that Bastet's greed was typical of *just* cat deities.

"I do not have enough knowledge to agree or disagree with you,

Mr. Tushman," Charon finally says. "And as usual, I find your question puzzling."

"For the millionth time, call me Larry. And fine, forget the cat analogy. You still didn't answer my questions. Who were you ferrying the day the gods left? Who was that last soul to squeak into Heaven—"

"Hell. Tartarus, to be exact," Charon corrects him as he sets his oar into the water.

"Fine—Hell. Who was he? Or she? How did that last ferry go before they … you know." Larry makes a whistling sound as he flutters his hands, mimicking a bird flying away.

"As I told you many times before, I cannot reveal the name of the last soul I ferried into Hell that day. To do so would break a sacred oath taken long before birds grew wings with which to fly."

Larry waves a dismissive hand. "I know, I know. Client-attorney privileges—I get it. I just figured the statute of limitations might have expired or something. I mean, so many of the rules have changed, and …"

"The rules have changed, but I have not, Mr. Tushman." Charon looks at the tiny island he is currently navigating toward. "Well, I have not changed as much as most."

"OK, one last question—"

"Mr. Tushman, correct yourself. Lying was the most common trait possessed by the souls I once ferried to Hell."

"It's a figure of speech, not a lie," Larry says.

"Figures within speech are poor representations of the truth."

"Fine, fine. One last question *today*."

Charon nods in approval.

"What do you think would have happened if the gods left while that soul was still on your boat?"

Charon pauses, his oar still in the water. He has never considered this before. A human soul is a complex construction; of all the energies ever created, nothing is more powerful than a soul.

But with great power comes great *limitations*. For one thing, a soul needs to be contained … it cannot exist in the ether, but must be tethered to a plane of existence capable of containing it.

That is *designed* to contain it.

Which is the very definition of Heaven or Hell: a plane of existence capable of holding a human soul.

"I suppose he would have dissipated to nothing. Faded away as his energy was absorbed into the only fabric of existence that remains: Earth. For that is what happens to the human souls now, once they are freed from their mortal coils. They dissipate into nothing. It is the only thing left for the human soul to do."

"Bleak," Larry says. "And also, that last soul was a *he*. Good to know."

Charon lifts a curious eyebrow.

"You mentioned that the last soul was a 'he.' In other words, you let a clue drop, narrowing down my search by fifty percent. I'm now that much closer to figuring out who that last soul to get in belonged to." Larry gives the ferryman a maniacal grin.

"Mr. Tushman, I ferried thousands of souls on that last day," Charon says. He is giving this persistent human more knowledge than what was once permissible—but as the human pointed out, the rules have changed. "That is the essence of my being: to be with all departed souls at all times. Back when the gods existed and my power was unlimited—and such a feat was possible—I could be, as you humans put it, in more than one place at once, with more than one soul at once, ferrying them all in tandem."

"How is that even possible?" Larry asks as he mulls over the power required to do such a thing.

Charon tilts his head. "Are you really going to risk your eternal soul for another question?"

Larry shrugs. "It's not like there's a Hell to be ferried to. So yeah, I think I'll risk it."

"It was my nature that allowed me to be with many souls at once."

"Cool, like in *Multiplicity*."

Charon tilts his head farther.

"Michael Keaton movie. Not very good. You didn't miss much," Larry says before his eyebrows furl in thought.

Charon knows what's coming … another question.

"You used the word 'nature' to describe how you could be with multiple souls at once. That's a very specific word to use. I mean, all living things have aspects that are their nature, but what you did was magical, and …" Larry's words trail off as he considers his question. "I guess what I'm asking is, what's the difference between nature and magic?"

Charon gives this AlwaysMortal an approving nod; he is sharper than most. "Magic is a force of will. Nature is what happens without my active participation. It was my nature to sense the newly departed souls on Earth that needed ferrying."

"And what about now? Does your nature still work?"

"Do you ask if I still feel the departure of souls that need ferrying?"

Larry nods.

"I do. I hear the cries of every soul who leaves this mortal plane, searching for their next place of being. But despite their cries, there is nothing I can do for them," Charon says with a heavy sigh. "There is nowhere I can ferry them to."

↔

And so Charon ferries living humans as he feels the dead depart. This continues for four long years, until one day Charon feels the cry of a soul that demands something he has never felt before.

This soul does not cry to be ferried to the afterlife.

This soul demands to be ferried back to Earth. Back to the mortal coil that once hosted its vast and unfathomable energy.

1
THREE DEAD GODS. THREE DEAD GODS

SEE HOW THEY RESURRECT ...

"This is all because of me?" I asked as I stood—well, not really stood, more like floated—in an impossibly dark room. And by dark, I don't mean that the lights were off, or even the kind of darkness you'd find in a coffin buried six feet under. I've been in both, and even in those situations you got the sense that *something* surrounded you—that light had, at one point, existed in that space.

This place felt as though it had never seen light and had no concept of what light could be. It was like being in the total absence of anything, and I was standing nowhere, in nothing.

Given that I was dealing with dead gods, my feeling probably wasn't far off.

"Yes. You have saved us," said the feminine voice. From what I knew about the dead gods, she would be Izanami, the Japanese goddess of creation who died not long after the world was created. "Because of your soul and the soul of one other, we can be free once again. For that we shall be forever in your debt."

Wonderful—three newly freed, maniacal gods in my debt. That was an obligation I wanted about as much as a tanuki's *cojones* to the face.

"Tell us, Katrina Darling, how shall we reward you? Perhaps you would like to rule the world?" said the deepest of the three.

"For us, of course," the three voices said.

"Or riches," said Izanami.

"Or power," said the many voices.

"I don't want any of those things," I said, trying to orientate myself. I looked behind me, but there was nothing to see other than the doorway I just walked through. It was illuminated by the light inside and hung open, revealing the museum's corridors that I had traversed to get to this place. "And might I ask who you are?"

None of the three voices answered.

"OK," I said, "you want to keep me in the dark, both figuratively and literally. I get it. Still, I learned a bit about you guys from Kenji, and—"

"Nurikabe traitor," the multi-voice creature hissed.

"—and I'm going to say the guy who sounds like everyone I've ever known—as in, ever—is Quetzalcoatl. I'm basing this on the part of your legend that mentions your death, when you were turned into a flock of birds. As in plural. The female voice is Izanami, but that was easy: she's the only girl here. Besides me, of course."

"How perceptive," boomed a male voice so deep it made James Earl Jones sound like a prepubescent kid. "Tell me, mortal without a soul, who am I?"

"Baldr," I said, "is that you?" I said it in the same tone one might use when hearing a long-lost friend's voice over the phone.

"Indeed. Indeed," he said between chortles of booming, thunderous laughter.

I tried to edge toward the doorway, but despite all my efforts, all I managed was to move my arms and legs without actually getting anywhere. The door was no closer, and I was beginning to feel like I was in one of those stress dreams where as hard as you might try, you never seem to get anywhere.

"You don't want any of those things, you say?" Baldr asked. "Then what is it that you do want?"

"My soul back," I said, turning my head in an effort to sense where the voice was coming from. No good; in a place where light had never existed, where I floated through space, the three gods' voices boomed around me like a thunderstorm.

"Ahh, that is the one thing we cannot grant you," the three voices said in unison.

"Why?" I asked. "If you're so grateful, then certainly I can have my soul back, can't I? I mean, by your own admission, you owe me."

"We do. But perhaps a more accurate statement is that we are in your debt *for giving us your soul*," said Izanami.

"Your soul and one other's," echoed Quetzalcoatl's flock of voices.

"Alright," I said, "I need you guys to spell this out for me."

"Death has different rules for different creatures," Izanami said. "When one of our creations dies, it becomes a spirit that may or may not continue to be."

I didn't miss that Izanami had referred to me—and the rest of humanity—as an "it." This didn't bode well for our continued negotiations.

"When a god dies, it presents merely a temporary limitation," boomed Baldr. "But when a human dies? Well, that is something special indeed."

As he spoke, I could feel my body rotating as if I was slowly spinning ... not around, but upside down. I looked back at the door—my only point of reference in this otherwise empty space—and saw that I had, indeed, flipped upside down. Not that "upside down" was a thing in a place with no floors, walls, or ceilings.

My slow rotation should have been disorientating, but it wasn't. Since my feet weren't attached to anything, it didn't actually feel like I was moving at all in this void.

Except that this place wasn't a void. Not exactly. If it was, I wouldn't be moving at all. Well, not without something propelling me, like a current or a breeze. Something, anything to push me along and actually cause me to rotate. This hall (room? cave? I'm going to go with cave ... that feels like the right word for big, dark and scary) was being affected by something that was causing me to move.

"Before the gods left," Izanami said, "death for those with souls was, in truth, the gift of everlasting life. Their souls would travel far, entering whatever heaven or hell their faith and gods dictated."

"But that was then," Quetzalcoatl said. "Now that those fickle, uncaring creators have abandoned their constructions for worlds unknown, death for humans is the final moment of everything."

"What a waste," Baldr said.

"A waste, for it is souls that power the gods' domains."

"It is the human soul that grants us our magic."

"Gives us strength."

"And it is your soul—"

"—and one other's—"

"—and one other's which have given us enough strength to rise once again," Quetzalcoatl hissed.

↔

The cave fell silent.

"Let me get this straight. My soul is … what? Your guys' battery?"

"If you mean 'well of power,' then yes."

"And you guys tried to kill me. Why?"

"To uncomplicate matters," Baldr said in a way-too-jovial tone, given that he was talking about my death. "After all, the body must die for the soul to be free."

"But your bodies don't die and your souls are free."

"An exception," Izanami said.

"An anomaly," agreed Quetzalcoatl.

"A vampire," I said. "Don't tell me you've never heard of us."

The three dead gods didn't say anything and I was beginning to think that they actually hadn't heard of vampires before. Like we were some sort of supernatural being that came into existence after these guys died.

If these guys died long enough ago, that was certainly possible.

Which made me wonder when vampires first came into existence. But that wasn't something I could think about now.

"You want to reward me for donating my soul? And that reward will take the form of an empire that I can rule over? That sounds like a lot of work. I'm more of a spa girl, myself."

"Then slaves?" Quetzalcoatl said.

"Or pleasures of the flesh?" Izanami offered.

"Or simple, forever-lasting joy?" Baldr boomed.

Another thing about powerful beings: they tended to believe you wanted to serve them simply because they were powerful. That somehow just being in their presence was reward enough. In other words, they didn't offer you power, glory or riches unless you had something they wanted.

Or they were afraid of you.

"Humph," I grunted, trying to think of a way to get more out of them. "So do I get to see you three guys, or do we keep chatting in absolute darkness like some twisted game of Seven Minutes in Heaven?"

This doesn't make sense, I thought (making sure it was in my head). *As best as I can tell, the nio and shisa guardians were sent by these guys—and not to offer me an invitation. They were trying to kill me. But here I am, standing in some perverse version of Plato's Cave (sans the roaring fire), being thanked by the very same gods who wanted me dead.*

"*Wanted* you dead," Izanami said with an inflection that implied that was no longer the case. "Now, we want you whole," she continued, confirming my suspicions.

"Hold on," I said, "I know I thought that in my head. How did you—?"

"We have your soul."

"And the soul knows all," Baldr boomed.

Great, I thought, *it was bad enough that I often think out loud. But now even my inside-thoughts are being aired for everyone to hear.*

"Not everyone," Quetzalcoatl said.

"Just us."

Creepy.

"OK." I sighed. "I would still like to see you. You know—get to know your names. Basic etiquette for the master-minion relationship."

"So you agree to serve us?"

"What choice do I have? Regardless, I would like to see you."

"Then see us," Izanami said, as if that explained everything.

I was just about to ask where the light switch was when I felt a pulsing, almost warm glow in my chest right where my heart was. And, to paraphrase the Big Guy, "Then there was light and it was … odd."

2

THE DARK SIDE OF YOUR SOUL

he room lit up. What lay around me was less Plato's Cave and more *Alice in Wonderland*. Standing (or floating; I wasn't really sure because I couldn't see their feet) before me were three figures who towered above me tenfold. Because I was floating at eye level less than twenty meters away, it was hard to capture all of their details. It felt kind of like looking at the tip of an iceberg: you just know there's a whole lot more below the surface.

Three figures—three dead gods—stood before me. At the center was Izanami-no-Minoto, the first and most obvious of the three. The gray, decaying flesh of her cheeks was peppered with giant holes big enough for minivans to drive through. Through those holes I could see the crimson-red lining of her gums, tongue and inner throat. Her left eye was being eaten by maggots the size of mountain lions and only patches of long black hair remained on her head.

She looked like an extra on *The Walking Dead*, but despite her zombie-like appearance, I could see the beauty she'd possessed before she died all those centuries ago. As she stared at me, she gripped the pendant on her necklace like a child trying to keep a toy from a playmate.

To her left stood Quetzalcoatl, his face more like a thunderbird you'd find at the top of a Native American totem pole than anything alive. Purple and gray lines framed his features, highlighting his eyes and nose. Where his ears should have been, two wings jutted straight out like the broken cowl on a Batman costume. If that wasn't weird enough, the ancient Aztec god didn't have a mouth. He had a beak—or rather *beaks*, as in plural. He had beaks. Hundreds of them. They were all normal-sized and belonging to all kinds of birds, from a long pelican's beak to a tiny sparrow's beak.

And finally there was Baldr, who was by far the easiest to look at because he just looked like a fat Norseman with a large, red beard and smile that betrayed uneven, off-white teeth. He looked quite … human. Well, if you discounted the fact that he was bigger than most skyscrapers and had an arrow sticking out of his chest. I guess that's what it takes to kill a god … a magical arrow the size of the CN Tower.

"So," I said, feeling very much like small Alice, "that wasn't weird at all."

Only Baldr seemed to get my attempt at levity, because he gave me a chuckle before booming, "Oh, my dear, weird is what we dead gods do."

"I'm getting that vibe," I said, taking a moment to look around. Other than the three gods, there didn't seem to be anything else in the room except a faint glow far, far below me.

What wasn't in sight was a jar holding my soul in it. But given how vast this place was and how little of it I could see, that jar could have been anywhere.

There was something else missing that I had expected to be here: my fear. Despite standing in front of three towering gods, I wasn't afraid. If anything, I was bored and mildly frustrated that they were here. I'd been accused of being a brazen fool, too stupid to know what was good for me, but a complete lack of fear in such overwhelming circumstances was strange, even for me.

I should have been cowering in fear. Or awe. But I simply wasn't.

Was this a side effect of not having my soul? I had been feeling empty—depressed, even. But my emotions hadn't been so muted that

I wasn't able to care about things … it was just getting harder and harder to do so.

But caring about your friends and being terrified that you could be swatted down like a fly were two different things. And right now, neither really bothered me.

"So," I said, fighting the urge to yawn, "now what?"

"Now we send you back," chorused Quetzalcoatl. Having a thousand beaks was one thing, but seeing them move in sync as they all spoke the same words was something else entirely. Worst choir ever.

"Send me back and …" I let the last word hang with the hope that they'd fill in the blanks.

Baldr took the bait. "And you wait for us as we gather our strength and emerge." As he said "emerge," he lifted a hand the size of five cruise ships docked on a medium-sized island.

The force of such a large mass in the void sent ripples that actually propelled me backward, tumbling head over heels. Although it was disorienting to move with such force against my will, I wasn't nauseated or dizzy. It was as if my inner ear was working overtime to make this feel … normal.

Normal or not, I didn't like moving against my will and I stuck out my arms to stop. That didn't do anything and now I was just tumbling with arms outstretched. Annoyed more than anything else, I thought about how much I'd just like to stop.

And I did. As soon as the word *"Stop"* fully formed in my mind, my body ceased moving, and I found myself hovering with my face pointed decidedly downward. And what's more, I had that same warm feeling in my chest.

"Oh," I said, "that's how this works." And focusing my gaze on the light beneath them, I shot down like an osprey hunting for fish.

↔

17

Back when I was a relatively young vampire—only eighty years old or so—I briefly dated a dark elf. There isn't a lot about my time with him that I care to remember. We were in a romance of evil bliss, two virtually indestructible creatures doing as they wished in both the mortal plane and the UnSeelie Court, and we did a lot I wish we hadn't.

And so, when I was floating in an empty void with three dead gods trying to hire me as their *numero uno* henchman (well, henchwoman), it felt somehow appropriate that I thought about him. More specifically, about what he'd taught me about magic.

You see, a vampire doesn't have magic. Sure, there were plenty of powers granted by magic, but those were part of the package, not something we could manifest out of nothing.

This always puzzled him and he spent many an evening training me in hopes that vampires did, in fact, have latent magical abilities. "Magic is the intersection of desire, will and faith," he used to say. "The desire to create an effect that isn't, the will to see it through and the faith that you are capable of doing it."

Despite all the desire, will and faith in the world, I never did manifest that magic. And he ultimately left me because I wasn't magical enough for him.

Well, if only he could see me now.

Staring at the light below, I formulated the desire to get closer as I focused my will on having it. And as for faith … well, three hundred years of battles and near-death experiences tend to be a confidence-builder.

I dove toward the light and as I did, I saw Baldr and Izanami's hands reach down to grab me. But they were huge and slow, and given their size it was like they were trying to swat a mosquito flying at near supersonic speed.

I easily dodged their clumsy hands and then I did something completely natural that had the most unnatural of effects. I muttered, "I wish these guys would just leave me alone." And just like that, they disappeared. I mean, one minute you're facing off against three titans so large they can be seen from space and the next second—poof … gone. Top that, David Copperfield!

Completely unfettered, I approached the light below. I didn't know what to expect when I got there; I was hoping it was my soul trapped in a jar and that all I had to do was pop open the lid and drink it back down into me like a Red Bull.

But Hope is a fickle bitch who rarely shows up dressed the way you want her to.

As I drew closer, I didn't see a jar or a ball of energy that could be my soul.

I saw an angel nailed to a cross, floating in the void. What's more, I recognized the creature from vids General Shouf had played for me back in the base on Okinawa.

"Shit," I said, stopping my flight next to the floating crucifix covered in the same symbols I'd seen on the shell the futakuchi-onna had left behind on the plane over. Whatever this cross was made of, it was covered with the symbols of renewed life that Deirdre had told me about. "Gabriel?"

The archangel turned a weary head in my direction before his lips turned slightly upward. "You made it, Ms. Darling. I guess some prayers are still answered in this GoneGod World."

3

WE ALL HAVE OUR ANGELS TO BURDEN

"I'm sorry," I said, shaking my head, "but you know my name?"

"I know the names of all, as I do their deeds, Ms. Darling," the archangel said.

Oh great, I thought, *his "thing" had to be that.*

Every angel had a "thing"—a special ability or purpose for which they were created. For some, it was power and authority, qualities they had in spades. Others had mercy or healing, and you'd be hard-pressed to find a creature capable of more empathy than an angel. I'd even heard of one whose "thing" was to know every written word, including those written on one's soul. Combine that with a supernatural memory, and that angel literally knew everything ever transcribed.

Up until the gods left, that was. After the GrandExodus, all the angels had lost their thing. But given that the gods had left four years ago, it meant that they weren't completely up to date, but weren't too far behind, either. Operating on Windows 7, so to speak.

And Gabriel's thing was knowing all my deeds. Not my thoughts, mind you, or any of my inner conflicts or internal debates. Just the final action I took on every little thing I'd done during my three hundred years of life. Given that the archangel Gabriel was generally regarded as a force for good, I was surprised he seemed happy to see me.

Like I've said before: during my time as a vampire, I did a lot of things I'm not proud of. And by "not proud of," I mean "spending the rest of my mortal life trying to make up for."

Not sure what to say, I floated there dumbly, waiting for the angel to say something—anything. But Gabriel just looked at me with a pained expression. From the way his arms hunched down and his body dragged, it seemed that gravity was pulling him down, causing him immense pain. That was something I could remedy, and I angled his cross so that he was lying down.

He shook his head and between gasped breaths, said, "Thank you, but I'm afraid there is no position in which my body does not drag down against these nine-inch nails. That is the design of the cross: to inflict pain, no matter what."

Well, that sucked. But given that I'd just vanquished three dead gods, I was starting to think I had unlimited power in this place. "Hold still," I said as I focused on the nails, willing them to pull out. But as hard as I tried, I couldn't get them to move.

"The gods' powers may be limited here, but they are not insubstantial. Only they can free me and I fear that is something they will never do. Not as long as I refuse to serve them," he said. "And as clever as your vanquishing may be, they shall return, Ms. Darling."

I looked around, but couldn't see anything coming, and I felt like I was deep in the ocean, below the line of light, waiting for a shark to swim into view. "I figured it was too easy. But they don't want to kill me, so what do I really have to worry about?"

"They only stay their hands because they do not know what will happen if a living body dies in a heavenly plane of existence." Gabriel strained his face in obvious pain as he spoke. Given that I had seen— as in, actually saw with my own eyes—Gabriel die during a firefight with a human army, the fact that he was here before me, tangible and in pain … well, that was all sorts of weird. I knew a lot about mythology and creatures of legend, a lot about the heavens and hells, and my eidetic memory allowed me to recall things in an instant (kind of like having Google's search engine for a brain—go nerdy me!), but even still, I had no idea how any of this was possible. Angels couldn't die ... could they?

"How is this possible? How are you here and not, you know ... wherever angels go when they die?"

"The light," Gabriel offered, letting out a long sigh. "But unlike humans, we do not go to the light—we become light. But that is not an answer to your question."

Finally! I thought. *An Other who actually acknowledges when they're being cryptic.* I waited patiently for the actual answer to the question I'd asked, thinking to myself that good things come to those who wait.

"For you ask the wrong question," he said.

GoneGod damn it! So much for good things and all that crap.

"The dead gods will return soon," the angel continued. "Even now I feel them gathering their strength as they approach. They seek to stop you and deny your claim to your soul. But they do not know how to stop your claim, and they fear killing you here will only strengthen that claim."

"Why?" I asked. "Why do they want my soul so badly?"

"Because human souls power this place. And it is with human souls that they can raise themselves once again. If you don't regain your soul and end their bid for resurrection, they will return and enslave the world. They only need time—seven days, by human measurement. Then they will be at full strength and unstoppable."

"Seven days, eh? Plenty of time to slay a god or two." I laced my words with as much sarcasm as I could muster.

If he caught my sarcasm, he made no indication of it. "You can end them today—this hour, even. Reclaim your soul and slay them one by one."

"Well, it is my soul," I said, a bit more childlike than I meant to sound. "And I do want it back."

"Indeed it is. That is why I asked the EverPresents to do what they must to aid you in your journey here. They, like me, traverse the world of the living and the dead. We are always linked in that way.

And even though they are of another … religion, when I told them of your mission they were eager to help."

"EverPresents?" Why couldn't Others use simple names? Everything had to be so damn cryptic with these guys. Still, the word "Ever-Presents" did give me a clue as to what he meant. "Do you mean the yokai that have been following me everywhere? The woman on the plane? The three ghost-kids in the parking garage on Okinawa? Do they have something to do with these symbols—which are Morrigan's runes, aren't they? You've been using the Red Queen's magic to bring the Others back to life. Well, half-life." I pointed at his cross.

Gabriel nodded. "It was the only way for me to help you. You needed to come here and claim your soul before …"—he let the word hang, and then sighed—"before the gods use it to regain themselves," he said, like that explained everything.

"You mean like coming back from the dead?"

"That is exactly what I mean."

I wanted to probe more, ask more questions, get more insight into how this whole damn universe was built, but if he was right, we were running out of time and they would be back any second. "OK, then what can I do?"

"Your soul … it is a source of great power, especially here. And because you live, you have a claim to it, but not necessarily control over it. You must make them acknowledge your claim before they gather further strength."

"Fine," I said, "I want my soul back, too. I really do. But I can't see it anywhere. I can't even sense it. How do I get it back?"

"Izanami carries the Soul Jar around her neck," he said, and I thought back to how she'd jealously gripped her necklace. Made sense she'd want to keep me away from that. "And the three gods share your soul and one other's … harnessing its power to control this domain. You have claim over your soul and only your soul. And your claim is greater than theirs. Retrieve your soul and destroy them."

"Excuse me?" I said.

"Retrieve your soul. Do it now, before their strength grows greater."

"OK," I said, flying backward in a loop—the floater's equivalent of nervous pacing. "Let me get this straight. You want me to cut out my soul that has been consumed by three separate and very dead gods?"

Gabriel winced as he nodded.

"Not to curse in front of an angel or anything, but the expression, 'There isn't a hope in Hell' comes to mind."

The archangel curled his lips slightly. "Actually, Hell is built on hope. For torment can only work when there is hope. And there is hope, Katrina Darling."

"How do you figure?"

"Despite everything that has happened to you, you are here, ready to do what is right. Therein lies the hope."

I groaned. "You're going to need more than that."

"I know," he said. "That is why I asked the EverPresent to deliver you the spearhead."

"Spearhead?" I said, thinking back to when I was attacked by the strange yokai who'd stabbed me with a spearhead on the plane. When the blade pierced my being, I'd thought I was done. As in game over, the end, walk into the light, done. But it turned out that both the yokai and the spearhead were ghosts, because as soon as the damn thing went into me, both the spearhead and the yokai had disappeared.

I nodded. "I don't know if I'd say she 'delivered' it. It was more like a stabbing motion. She did call it a 'gift', but in my experience gifts tend to be wrapped in boxes, not inserted in bodies. Besides, as soon as she drove it into my gut, both she and the spearhead disappeared."

"Excellent, then you have the Lance of Longinus with you now?" He looked visibly relieved.

"Sorry, did you say the Lance of Longinus? As in, the spear that pierced the side of Jesus?"

"Yes, it is the only thing that can kill a god and—"

But before Gabriel could finish, the three dead gods appeared before me.

24

4
THESE GODS AIN'T SO TOUGH

*T*he gods had abandoned their I'm-bigger-than-Godzilla intimidation tactics for something smaller. All three were now my size, which is to say, five-foot-nothing and a hundred and one pounds of fun. That in and of itself was a bit odd, because you'd think they'd go for something a little bigger than me. But even Baldr, with his massive beer belly, had shrunk to a my-size level.

"You," Quetzalcoatl echoed, "dared." He lifted his hand up and several ravens manifested before him, darting out at me. The carrion scavengers dove at me, using their powerful talons and sharp beaks as slashing and piercing weapons.

If they hadn't been trying to kill me before, they certainly weren't following the same tactic now.

The birds ripped through my flesh and it hurt. But the thing about me and pain: I'd been stabbed and shot enough times as a vampire to know what kind of threat I was under. I'd also done enough of my own slashing and piercing to know when a wound was fatal. And as painful as these attacks were, none of the ravens actually did that much damage. Certainly not as much as they should have been doing, given how many they were.

But the strangest part was that with every attack, my wounds healed almost instantly. It seemed in this plane of existence, I was a less-hairy Wolverine.

As fun as it was to watch deep cuts stitch up in a matter of seconds, there were bigger gods to fry. I reached out and plucked one of the ravens out of the ether, ripping it apart before grabbing another. Picking them off one by one was going too slow and just as I was wishing I had a giant net to catch them all with, I felt a large wooden handle manifest in my hands.

I looked at what I was holding and realized that some wishes do come true; I had a giant butterfly net. With a twist of my wrist, I caught the flock with an ease that simply shouldn't have been possible.

Not that I had much time to revel in my victory, because Baldr, seeing me unimpeded by the ravens, manifested two throwing daggers and chucked them at me. I managed to twirl Gabriel round so that the daggers stuck into the back of the cross.

Using Gabriel as a human—or rather, angelic—shield, I cowered behind his cross as I considered my next move. "This is going way too easily," I remarked to the pinned archangel.

"They do not have the power to end you in this domain," Gabriel said, "but that will not always be the case. Should they actually rise, they will be undefeatable. Please, Ms. Darling, end them now. This day. This battle."

I peered over Gabriel's cross and saw that the three gods had huddled together. From the panic in their eyes and the way they rapidly spoke to each other, I could tell they were worried.

Frightened, even.

"OK," I said, "how?"

"The spearhead. Conjure it and end them. Then, before they can raise themselves again, carve out your soul from their carcasses and end them once more by severing their heads from their bodies. Once that is done, be sure to draw and quarter them, sending their body parts to opposite ends of this world and any other world you have access to."

"That was … specific," I said, blinking twice as I stared at the suffering archangel. "But I already told you: I don't have the spearhead."

"You do—it is within you. Draw it forth and—"

But before he could finish advising me on how to summon a god-killing spearhead that was apparently inside me, a shadow somehow loomed over us in a lightless room. I looked up to see a massive paper fan coming down at us.

I knew enough of Izanami's legend to know this was the fan she had used to vanquish demons before she died. Gabriel and I may not have been demons, but we were still vanquishable.

Izanami brought down the giant paper fan (I wish I was kidding) and swatted us like flies. Since there was no ground to be swatted against, we wound up tumbling down to nothing.

I guessed that meant they were done with the "Will you be my minion?" strategy.

↔

A new flock of birds flew from the void below, but instead of physical representations that pierced and cut, these guys flew through us. Sort of. Because as each one entered our beings and flew out the other side, they seemed to take with them a wee bit of us.

It felt as though I was being carried away, bit by bit.

Gabriel's words confirmed this when he cried out, "They're trying to weaken you piece by piece."

"In other words, they're doing unto us what you told me to do unto them." I hit the "untos" hard in hopes the archangel appreciated my biblical vernacular.

But all the archangel did was nod. So much for trying to speak the lingo.

I wasn't sure how to stop them, and I thought about how this was a lot of trouble for a soul. But it was more than my soul, wasn't it? This was about me being whole again, and these guys were literally causing the opposite of what I had come here to achieve.

This shouldn't have been happening. Not here, and not with the kind of power this place granted me. Remembering who I was—the complete, unabridged version of myself—I imagined my body as a magnet, drawing into it all the pieces that were being cut away.

I will never doubt the power of imagination again—not after what happened next. The pieces of me that had been ripped away weren't just returned to me … they came barreling out of the birds like lead balls being ripped straight from their insides.

The birds died by the hundreds, but because this place had no gravity, they just hung in the sky like dead, hole-filled carcasses.

Quetzalcoatl screamed in pain as his birds died, and from the way he screamed, I guessed they weren't just constructs, but actual pieces of him.

Seeing the god writhe in pain, I suddenly knew two things.

I was going to win.

And they weren't.

5

WHO'S SAVING WHO?

*G*abriel must have sensed the same thing, because he cried out, "Finish them here and now. Finish them before they have a chance to manifest themselves and throw the world into darkness. Finish them and reclaim what is rightfully yours!"

"Hell yeah!" I screamed.

The archangel winced.

"Ahh, sorry. I meant, Heaven yeah! Now what did you say I needed again?" I snapped my fingers as if trying to remember something. "Oh yeah, the god-killing spearhead of the Lance of Longinus. Now where could that be hiding?"

"It is within you."

"I know," I said, rolling my eyes. "I was being rhetorical."

Placing a hand over my chest, I imagined where the futakuchi-onna had stabbed me. I imagined the spearhead within me and that all I needed to do was draw it out. And as I formed the imagine of the spear that stabbed Jesus, I felt a warm glow inside me.

Opening my eyes, I looked down and saw the spearhead slowly draw out of me. It was weird-looking: the bronze tip exited my body from a wound that did not bleed and, lifting up my shirt, I saw that my flesh hugging its sharp edges like sand filling the empty space of a hole.

Within seconds, the spearhead was withdrawn. Brandishing it at the dead gods, I mused, "This won't do, will it?" And I imagined a long wooden shaft on which I could mount it.

And you guessed it: a perfectly whittled, splinter-free shaft grew out of the spearhead right into my grip.

"Ahh," I said, "now that's much better."

↔

What do dead gods and cornered animals have in common? More than you'd think. These dead gods were screwed and they knew it. That's why I wasn't surprised by what happened next.

The second the spear manifested in my hands, the three gods threw everything they had at me. I mean *everything*.

Bolts of lightning and flashes of daggers flew from Baldr's hands as thousands of flesh-eating birds flocked toward me in a torrent of desperate squawks. Izanami conjured a dozen raijin and shikome—the same monsters she'd used to chase her husband Izanagi-no-Mikoto the day he tried to escape her tomb.

I was being bombarded by every ounce of power these guys had to muster and I swatted aside what they threw at me like a bug zapper in a swarm of mosquitoes. Between the spear and my heightened abilities deflecting everything, I'd never had an easier fight.

And still they continued their onslaught.

"End them now, Katrina," Gabriel shouted over the chorus of chaos in the void. "End them. Reclaim your soul. Save your world from the end of everything."

Ignoring the dead angel's commands, I focused on my soul, willing it to show itself. Sure enough, I saw three warm spots glowing within their chests and I knew Gabriel's words to be true: they really had divided up my soul, consuming a piece of it each.

Izanami, with her devil raijin, hovered closest. She would be the first to fall, the first to return to me what she had denied me. Pointing the Lance of Longinus at her heart, I charged forward. Another few feet and I would be upon her.

Another few feet and a piece of my soul would be returned.

But before the spear's tip could pierce her body, I felt something latch onto my back, pull me out of the void and back through the open doorway that led into Kami Subete Hakubutsukan's halls.

End of Part 1

PART II
INTERMISSION

6

CHARON

COMETH THE FERRYMAN

*N*EW YEAR'S EVE—

Most psychopomps can be anywhere in the known universes in an instant.

For most psychopomps, such travel is not conscious, but rather guided by the needs of the souls they must usher from the world of the living to that of the dead. And even stranger still, most psychopomps can be in many places at once, for death is great and the dying are many, and the lost souls' need for guidance is relentless.

Such is the power of psychopomps, the creatures whose sole purpose is to guide the dead. Certainly this is true of shinigami, epona, yama, xolotl, the Grim Reaper and the many, many other Others who reigned over the in-between places where the living had to traverse toward the Land of the Dead.

Such is the lot of psychopomps, the gods' death guides. But despite all that power, despite all that ability to traverse domains which even the gods were oft forbidden to enter, despite all the knowledge they possess, Charon still finds himself sitting in Vancouver Airport, waiting to board one of the humans' flying contraptions toward an island that divides the Pacific Ocean to the east from the China Sea to the west.

↔

"Do you have to go?" asks Larry as he carries Charon's luggage through the terminal. Not that Charon has "luggage"—his single possession is a lamp that Larry, using his mortal knowledge, carefully enveloped in a substance called bubble wrap and placed inside a sturdy cardboard box.

Besides his lamp, Charon only carries his walking stick, which grants him handicapped status in this GoneGod World and thus affords him preferred parking and shorter lines.

"I mean, it's New Year's Eve. Can't this wait until, I don't know, the New Year?" Larry's eyes tell the psychopomp that his question is not rhetorical. That, and the AlwaysMortal is willing to wait a long, long time for an answer.

But Charon does not understand the question. He is the guide whose boat carried the souls of Heracles, Aeneas, Hermes, Odysseus, Theseus, Sisyphus, and perhaps most famously, Virgil and Dante. But these are just a few; Charon has ferried countless others. And in each case, he *only* goes where he must.

Still, this AlwaysMortal was kind enough to usher him to the airport, kind enough to lend him use of his credit card (the mortal's equivalent of two copper pieces placed over one's eyes) and now carries his lamp.

"The dead do not care what festival Father Time has ordained the hour to be. This soul needs me now, so it is now that I must go," he says simply.

"And again: why?"

Charon lifts a confused eyebrow—a gesture he has picked up from his human friend. "A soul needs my guidance."

Larry considers his next words carefully. "But there is nowhere for the souls to go. I mean, didn't you tell me that they just kind of float off to …"—the human pauses as the thought catches in his throat—"Well, to nowhere?"

"True for most," Charon says. "But this particular soul languishes in Oblivion under special circumstances."

"And by 'Oblivion,' you mean the Land of the Dead?"

Charon nods. "Yes—in one of them, at least."

↔

Larry leaves him at the end of a fast-moving line called Immigration. There, several AlwaysMortals dressed in black question fellow travelers with the same vigor that St. Peter once did those who wished to enter Heaven's pearly gates.

But these gatekeepers question with far less mirth than Paul. It seems that granting one civil entry is a lost art in this world.

Charon is next, and this AlwaysMortal gatekeeper looks the psychopomp up and down before requesting, in a curt tone, that he give up his cane to be stowed in something called "luggage." Charon will not. In all of eternity, he has never been without it. If the gods could not separate him from it, what hope does this mortal have?

Charon eyes the security guard, answering with a heavy sigh that has silenced kings and unsettled saints alike. This audible cue imposes on the AlwaysMortal he is dealing with, and the security guard, eyes widening, nods in fear and submission.

With trembling hands, the guard says, "You'll have to stow it in special holdings once you're on the plane, I think." And lets him through with cane and lantern in tow.

As he walks to his gate, he hears the security guard groan, "I just met death ... and lived."

Barely, Charon thinks. *Barely, indeed.*

↔

Once inside the metal boat that flies in the sky, Charon extends his senses. The soul he seeks is trapped, held hostage by ... gods. Charon's eyes widen as the word swims in his mind. Gods. They still exist?

Charon does not understand what his instincts are telling him. He only knows them to be true. But if they are truly gods, then they must know they are defying one of the principles of life and death set before the first creature ever created breathed its first breath. No one —be it the gods or the Principles of Creation or nature—may possess a soul against its will.

To break such a rule would be to challenge the very fabric of reality, and such a challenge could shatter ...

Charon's thoughts stall as he searches his vast well of knowledge for the right word. It does not take long for him to finally settle on one: Everything.

Such a challenge could shatter everything.

In all of time, no god has ever dared such an insult to creation. But gods are gods; their arrogance and power imbue them with the false sense that they are above the law, be it a law of nature or the celestial laws ordained by the truly divine.

Charon receives his mineral water and leaves it unsipped on the tray. Such arrogance unsettles the guide to the dead, for his lot may be death, but even death is not the end. And these gods with their careless actions threaten to go beyond death and head-first into that very end.

Charon grits his teeth as he considers what he must do. He may only be a psychopomp, a servant to both mortals and gods alike, but there is one aspect of his nature that sets him apart from his counterparts. For when the gods imbued him with life and purpose, they granted one ability above and beyond those possessed by his counterparts.

And this power is so unusual, so great, that even the gods' departures could not deny him.

For if death is a river, then its current flows only one way; its rapids allow those who ride its waves only one direction of travel: from life to death. For once a soul travels into the light of death, it cannot return.

No being, human or Other, can traverse against death's relentless course.

From life to death.

Such is the universe's design.

From life to death.

But even the harshest rules set by the most uncompromising of creatures have exceptions. And that exception is Charon.

In all of existence and creation, only Charon can travel both ways.

Only Charon can guide this living soul away from the light of death and toward the darkness that is life.

↔

Charon knows what he must do, and an unfamiliar emotion washes over him. It is an emotion he has never experienced before, and as he wills this metal, flying boat to traverse the skies faster, he knows what he is feeling.

Charon—the psychopomp who came into existence the moment the first of the gods' creations died, the Other who has helped millions of anxious souls on their most vital and very final journey, and who has spent nearly his entire existence trawling the same course along the same river—is impatient.

ABSOLUTELY APOCALYPTIC
MISTAKES

ow —

"No," I screamed as I was pulled away from a battle that I'd been winning. "What ... are ... you ... doing?!"

"Saving your ass," Jean said as he dragged me away from the open doorway.

I pushed the soldier away with a swift kick to his chin and dived for the doorway that was only a few yards away. But before I could get inside, it closed and locked. Still, I knew that they couldn't keep me out of the void; this was just a stalling tactic while they regrouped.

Fumbling with the door handle, I turned to the stockpile of impossibly powerful items, looking for something, anything to burst through the door. But before I could even gather my thoughts, Jean was on me again.

"Come on," he said, "we've got to get out of here."

"No," I said, pulling away from him, "I have to get back into that room. I have to—"

"This place is going to blow and take anyone in here with them."

"You set the charges?"

Jean nodded.

"Turn them off!"

"I can't."

"You fool, do you know what you've done? You've killed us all!" I screamed, my voice getting shrill and panicky as I desperately tried to find a solution to an otherwise impossible situation. I pulled away, seeking to kick open the door and get back into the void. Maybe the godlike powers I'd had in that room were what I needed to stop what was about to happen.

Maybe if—

But before I could take two steps, I felt a sharp needle pierce the back of my neck just as the world around me faded to black.

↔

One moment I was in the Kami Subete Hakubutsukan's halls, desperate to get back into the void. The next I was in one of the island's thick tropical forests, laying on the ground as Keiko wiped sweat from my forehead.

And for one blissful moment, I forgot where I was, forgot where I had just been. For one blissful moment, I thought everything was OK.

But it seems that whenever I have a peaceful moment, it's usually followed by a crash.

I jolted up as the memory of everything that just happened rammed its way back into my head. And man, did that ever give me a headache.

I set a hand to my pounding forehead. "We've got to … we've got to get back. I have to kill those gods." The words sounded ridiculous to me, even after living through it. But if everything Gabriel had said was true, then I really did have to get back there. I really did have to kill those gods … again. And I really did have to get my soul back.

41

"We can't."

Turning, I saw Jean looking at his tricorder-like device, shaking his head. "We really screwed this one up," he added, not looking up from the screen.

"*We* screwed this up? *We* did?" I said, rising to my feet. "If it wasn't for you, *we* would be fine. I would have my soul back and those assholes would be … would be … well, they *wouldn't* be!" I cried out in exasperation.

"Excuse me," Jean said, looking up from his tricorder for the first time. "I think the words you're looking for are, 'Thank you,' and, 'I owe you my life.'"

That really pissed me off. I took two long strides before knocking the ridiculous device out of his hands. "I had it under control. I was winning and—"

"It didn't look like you were winning. It looked like you were in the middle of a tsunami of godly shit. I mean, I had to ignore some pretty amazing stuff to find you … and when I did, what did I see? Flocks of birds, giant fans, laser beams. As far as I could tell, Miss Ex-Vamp, you were about to die."

"I wasn't. Despite what it looked like, I was winning."

"Sure you were," Jean said. "Regardless, it's all water under the bridge. We need to—"

"Water under the bridge? *The bridge*? We're facing three evil gods coming back to life and you're throwing clichés at me? I was winning!" I cried out. "I was. And you cocked it up because you couldn't leave things well enough alone. I mean, why did you walk in there in the first place? You were meant to wait outside."

"Like you were meant to lock the place using that magical thread?"

"Gleipnir chain," I growled.

"Whatever. All I know is that I'm not the only one who has trouble following the plan."

That did it. Funneling as much water onto the bridge as I could, I yelled, "Look here, you sanctimonious prick. I knew damn well what I was meant to do. I also knew what it was going to cost me—my soul.

As much as you've learned to live without yours, I want mine back. I saw a chance and I went for it."

"More like you got greedy and stupid and would have gotten yourself killed if it wasn't for …" He cocked a thumb at himself.

"Let me guess," I said, "in this scenario, you think that you're some knight in shining armor who saved the damsel in distress, right? Two things about that. One, I was never in distress. And two, you aren't a knight. You're a mutha—"

"Katrina, Jean … please," Keiko said. Well, not so much said as growled. There was something in her tone and the authority it carried that caused me to stop. The noro priestess had gravitas. No wonder Others came to her beck and call.

"We are in a state of crisis," she continued. "Mistakes have been made. Choices, too," she quickly added, looking at me. "And now we must live with both. The path forward is not to question how we got here, but rather what we must do now that we are here."

"Wisely said," I said, giving Jean my best death stare. "We need to get me back inside as quickly as possible. I have…"—I searched for the word—"powers—I mean, incredible powers—in there."

"What kind of powers?" Jean asked.

"I don't know. I could manifest my will. It was like everything I thought came to be."

"Like Green Lantern." Jean smirked.

"Sure," I said, rolling my eyes. "Like Green Lantern, except I could also fly, had super speed, strength—"

"Like Superman."

Ignoring him, I added, "And I could think."

At this, Jean chuckled. "Unusual state of being for you, huh?"

I gave him the finger. "Funny, guy."

"Like I said, I'm hilarious in Paradise Lot."

"You know what it's like in the heat of battle. For the most part, you're going on instinct, reacting to what's happening on some subconscious level. But you're not thinking. Not really. That's why experience is so vital for a fight. Experience is the after-thoughts you had from previous fights kicking in and informing your instincts during the next one.

"But that wasn't the case in the museum. There, I was calm, peaceful. Calculating. Despite the chaos going on around me, I could assess the threats and react accordingly."

"Like Batman." Jean tilted his head. "So, you were basically the Justice League all wrapped into one until I screwed it up for you."

I nodded.

Jean pursed his lips as he lifted his face up toward the sky. "So, that's the good news," he said. "What's the bad news?"

"Good news?" I asked.

"Yeah. Well, I figure what's coming is going to be so horrible that me sticking my nose in where I shouldn't have will sound like the good part after you're done talking."

I have to hand it to him: when he's right, he's right, I thought. And from the way they looked at me, I knew I had said that out loud. But it was a natural enough thing to say, given what was going on, that neither of them seemed to notice I had meant to say it only in my head.

"OK," I sighed, "here we go ..."

I told them everything. About Gabriel and how the gods were using my soul (and the Raspy Man's soul, too) to resurrect themselves. That the gods only needed seven days to gain full power on Earth and given that the Celestial Solace was meant to last for a lot longer than that, meant they would have plenty of time to gather their powers.

I also pointed out—and not in an I-told-you-so manner, might I add—that locking the museum's door (as in, our original plan) would have only given the gods all the unbothered time they needed to raise themselves once again.

"And that's why I need to get back there," I said, "as soon as possible. I've got to face off against them and end them before they gain more power. Not that I'm sure I can. I don't have the Lance of Longinus anymore. It's in the void, I think, and I'm sure the gods aren't going to just leave it sitting around for me to stab them with it."

"That it?" Jean asked, and not in a cocky, I-got-this kind of way. It carried more of a please-let-that-be-it-because-I-don't-think-I-can-handle-more vibe to it.

I nodded, before remembering one last detail. "Also—and Gabriel made this perfectly clear—they need seven days to rise. Given that it all started today, we've still got seven days to deal with this. That may seem like a long time, but as much as I like to procrastinate, this is one assignment I'd like to hand in early, because if they do rise—in other words, leave the museum—we are screwed. As in, royally."

They listened and when I was done speaking, they both looked at each other as if they didn't want to tell me what was clearly running through both their minds.

"Spill it," I said.

Keiko gave Jean a nod, and with a heavy sigh, the soldier looked at me and said, "Let me put it this way: all that stuff you just told us … that's the good news."

↔

Jean picked up his tricorder thingy and handed it to me. "First off, we don't have seven days. We've got five."

"How do you figure? Gabriel was pretty clear that we had seven Earth days to get this done and since I was only in there for an hour at most, then we still have—"

"I'm starting to think that time must work differently in there, because you were gone for almost two."

"Hours?" I said with false hope.

"Days," Jean said.

I thought back to the discussions I'd had with both the gods and Gabriel, and the fight. It had all happened so fast that when I'd said an hour, I was being generous. It felt more like ten minutes. I tilted my head in confusion. "You mean to say that I was in there for two days? Two whole days?"

"Well, forty-five hours, but I'm a rounder-upper kind of guy, so …" He lifted two fingers.

"But …" I let my disbelief linger.

"You know," Jean said, "when you think about it, it kind of makes sense that time would be different in the Other domains. I mean, God —as in the big guy, capital 'G' God—supposedly created everything in seven days, but the Earth is millions of years old. So, if a day for the big guy is a couple million years for us … well, you get the point."

I groaned in comprehension as something Aki said came crashing back to me. The tanuki had pointed out that celestial domains rotate every few hundred days, and then made some vague point about eternity being locked into a second. At the time, I didn't understand what he'd meant. But with the new context of my two-day absence, I guessed that eternity really could reside in a second or two.

Shaking off the not-inconsiderable desire to debate the meaning of time over a piña colada, I said, "OK, so we have less time than I thought, but we can—"

"Sorry," Jean said, lifting a hand, "that was still part of our good news. And there's one more piece of good news I need to share with you."

Keiko groaned in frustration. "Great news, really," she said through gritted teeth. "All thanks to our American soldier friend and his toys."

Jean shrugged. "We all have to get our kicks from somewhere."

I shot him an impatient look.

"OK, OK. When we were getting you out of there, I decided to cover our tracks with a little bit of Cave Remodeling, Home Edition. In layman's terms, I set off a crap-ton of C4 in there."

Of all the things he could have said, that was absolutely the last thing I needed to hear. "What? How? When?" The words came out in rapid-fire exasperation.

"Well, you have to understand that when you actually got inside, the nio and shisa guardians stopped fighting us. Hell, they stopped everything and just stood there like the statues they were. I had some time, and you know what they say … 'Idle hands are the devil's playground.' I un-idled my hands by planting some bombs."

"Ah-ha," I said. "You collapsed the passageways. Maybe—" I cut myself off as I looked at the magical tattoo on my arm. It was something I'd gotten when looking for a way into the museum and it had done its job, leading us through a complex network of underground tunnels and right to the museum's front door.

Since being forcibly removed from the celestial tourist spot, I hadn't checked if my tattoo was still "active." I rolled up my sleeve and took a look. Familiar blue and orange lines ebbed and flowed on my forearm, with a red dot situated on the underside of my wrist: the museum.

But unlike before, where there was a clear path in, now the orange and blue lines just stopped and there was a three-inch gap between the edge of the lines and the entrance.

"Anything?" Keiko asked.

I shook my head. "Seems he did a thorough job," I said, the desperation of the situation weighing down on me. We had to get inside and we were running out of time. "So, we figure a way in," I growled. "More bombs, get a troop of dwarves or hire a team of those rami …"

"Ramidreju," Jean said.

"Yeah, those," I said snapping my fingers. "They can tunnel us in. Hell, we could even ask some Others to burn a few days of time to teleport me in. I'm sure there'd be a few willing to sacrifice a bit of life to avoid enslavement—"

"Yeah, so, about that," Jean said. "The good news is that there's already a crew of Others digging through the debris as we speak."

From the way he'd said it, I gathered that wasn't good news at all. "Let me guess: the bad news is that they're on Team Dead Gods Rising."

Jean gave me an appraising look. "Good name. And yeah, they're pretty rah rah for the gods. We're not getting inside. Not without a fight."

"So we fight."

"You don't get it. We'll need an army to get through." He made an exaggerated show of looking behind me. "Seems you forgot yours."

"What about yours?"

"Already called it in."

"And?"

"They're on their way."

"Excellent."

Jean shook his head. "I guess since we've gotten through all the good news, it's time to give you the bad news."

"Bad news? I thought you were just trying to bring a wee bit of levity to the situation. You mean to tell me that there's some actual bad news?"

Jean gave me a look that I imagined he used just before shooting someone in the head. A combination of apology, regret and you-had-it-coming. "So, remember that little army of Others that attacked the base before we got here? Well, they're here and they're definitely on Team Dead Gods Rising."

↔

Jean pulled out his tricorder, clicked a bunch of buttons that brought up satellite imagery of Okinawa. "This is the military's version of Google Earth. Same concept and functionality, except we can zoom in close enough to see that freckle on your nose."

A few more clicks and he zoomed in on our location. "We're here," he said, "and over here is the Celestial Solace Hotel where the hole first appeared."

The image showed an aerial view a few hundred feet above the hotel, and there I saw what he'd meant by "an army of Others." There were valkyries, angels, minotaurs, centaurs, sednas, chamroshes, wondjinas and baku and dozens of other Others. Hell, the resolution was so good that I could even see the hairy toes on a hobbit and the glitter a pixie farted out.

And of course, swooping about over the hotel was a whole flight of dragons. They comprised every color of a very deadly rainbow.

"Hey," I said, touching a little point in the rock garden, "can you zoom in closer over there?"

Jean clicked the screen twice and we saw, in full HD, a makeshift thatch-roofed prison with dozens of Others inside. Others like Harry and Aki. "Great. Our only allies, as few as they are, are P.O.Ws."

"Actually, I think they're just prisoners," Jean clarified. "I mean, given that they're not military, you can't really classify them as prisoners of war. Maybe human shields. Well, Other shields—"

"Yeah, because that's the point."

"Hey, words matter."

"You're an idiot," I said.

He put a hand over his heart. "Words also hurt."

I considered punching him in the nose to show him how fists hurt, but that would have just been a time-wasting distraction. And given we had little of that, my better angels overrode that urge.

"Continue with the bad news."

"Ahh yes, that ..." he said, rubbing his hands through his hair. It was more than a nervous gesture; he was also upset. Angry, even. "I tried to explain to my superiors what was happening. Told them everything except your part in this. It was already a lot for them to swallow without adding, 'There's this soulless girl who needs access to the museum.' Anyway, the boys with brass decided that they're going to launch a full-on assault. To put it simply, they're the Empire and they're readying their Death Star for a decisive strike against the rebel scum. We're supposed to get off the island ASAP."

"They're going to nuke this place?"

"They've done it before." Keiko's wry tone betrayed raw, unbridled anger.

Jean shook his head. "I know we're splitting hairs, but they're not going to nuke this place—just drop enough megatons of bombs to kill every animal, plant and Other on the island."

"It's not going to work," I said. "All the bombs in the world won't kill a god." *Much less three gods,* I thought. "We need to stop them."

He tossed me his communicator. "They won't listen to me. And before you say it, I have it on good authority that they've pre-written

49

my eulogy in case of my untimely death in the line of duty. They're going to bomb this place regardless of where my or your physical asses are located."

"Of course they are," I said. "What about the noro community on the island? They're going to kill them, too?"

As soon as I'd said it, my mind flew to Blue, and my chest clenched. Seems once you love someone, you never stop worrying about them.

Jean shook his head. "Actually, that's our rendezvous point and the only reason why this place hasn't seen the full fury of their wrath yet. They've sent a few boats to get the priestesses off the island. Once evacuation is done, then ..." He whistled a bomb dropping.

"We're screwed," I said. "They bomb the hell out of this place, stopping us from stopping the gods. They'll rise from their tombs and enslave the world. We are literally dead people walking."

"Yeah, you're right. I know you're right. But I'm out of options. They won't listen to reason because they don't believe in gods anymore—gone, dead or rising." Jean lowered his head in exasperation. Then he chuckled to himself. "That's not exactly true, what I said."

"Which part?"

"The options part. I have one option and it's a pretty good one. Go home, hug my wife and not let go until our overlords arrive. But even then, I doubt I'll let go. You know, cold dead hands and all." Jean was serious. That was exactly what he intended to do.

"It can't end like this. It can't. There's got to be another way. There's got to be something—anything—we can do."

"There is one more option," Keiko said, standing from the fallen log she had been sitting on. Her face showed resolve and deep contemplation as she considered her options. "It will mean breaking a sacred pledge I have taken as a noro priestess, but it may also mean salvation." A single tear fell from her eyes. "There is one who may help us. He is a being of considerable power and we noro have offered him sanctuary. We have also sworn that we would never ask anything of him. That he could live the rest of his time in peace. This was our oath to him … an oath I am willing to break."

Others and their oaths. They took them very seriously, and so too did their proxies. No matter how good Keiko's intentions were, to break an oath would mean ex-communication from her noro home.

Still, when the alternative was no home at all … well, therein lies human practicality.

I nodded deeply at her sacrifice, knowing that if she had offered to do this, she had already thought long and hard and made up her mind. "Right now the only option we have is to ask," I said. "Who is he?"

"Chronos."

"The Titan?" Jean and I asked in unison.

"They're still around?" I asked, giving Jean an *I got this* look. If anyone was going to express exasperated confusion, it was going to be me.

Keiko shrugged. "I don't know anything about the Titans … and you're thinking Cronos. I'm talking about Chronos."

Sadly, as is oft the case in the GoneGod World, clarification only served up more questions. "And he is …?" I eventually said.

The noro priestess pursed her lips and then, without a hint of irony or humor, said, "Father Time."

8

TWO ROADS DIVERGED IN A YELLOW WOOD

"There's an Other called 'Father Time?' " I asked in disbelief.

"He isn't an Other exactly," Keiko said. "And to call him an Other is strange. It is like calling a lion a cat. Or a zombie a human. He is more of the physical representation of the *concept* of time than anything else."

I had heard of these creatures before … Others so powerful that they weren't created by a god, but rather came into being as the laws that governed the universe began to establish themselves. Even the gods feared them.

"And he lives here?" Jean asked.

Keiko nodded. "After the gods left, we had many travelers come to our island for sanctuary. Most wound up living in Celestial Solace Hotel, finding refuge there. But some of particular power and ability asked for seclusion and separation from the rest of the world. They did so because they feared that they would be seen as the new gods in this GoneGod World. Others, because they are creatures of such immense power that they did not wish to be used by humans or Others alike for purposes that did not align with their desires."

"And Father Time is one of them."

Keiko nodded.

"Who else?" Jean asked.

Keiko narrowed her eyes in suspicion by way of an answer.

Jean lifted his hands. "Hey, I'm only asking in case Father Time says no. I mean, if you have another Other there that could be of use, don't you think we should play the field a bit?"

"No," Keiko said with finality. "Father Time is the only one I believe can help, and thus the only one with whom I am willing to break my oath."

"But there might be another who—"

"Jean," I said, "I've seen that look on her grandmother's face before. There isn't a force in this world or any other that will get her to budge, so cut your losses and move on." Turning to Keiko, I added, "So let's go speak to Father Time." I gestured for Keiko to lead the way.

↔

Keiko took the lead as we walked through the thick brush in silence, and Jean walked far enough behind that he was ... what? Dilly-dallying, watching our rears? I really had no idea why he was so far behind. Not that I cared; as far as I was concerned, the farther away he was, the better.

Keiko must have sensed my anger, because she subtly slowed her pace so that before I knew it, I was basically walking next to her. When our strides finally matched up, she put a hand on my shoulder. "You know, you are being unduly harsh on the soldier behind us. You were gone a long time. At first the nio and shisa were content to just stare across the bridge, like unmoving, unthinking sentries. But something happened and they started to—"

"Attack you and Jean again?"

Keiko shook her head. "No, I believe they were trying to stop you from escaping. One moment they were still, the next, frantic. Desperate, even, as they tried to get across the chasm. Many fell to their deaths, but the few that managed to jump across immediately turned their power against the door, as if they were trying to destroy the entrance ... or, rather, your exit."

I thought about this, and from what I knew, that move made sense. I was winning against the gods and up until I produced the spear, the three dead gods and I had been in a stalemate, with neither side able to kill the other.

Certainly I wasn't under any threat of death, and the best the gods could hope for was trapping me inside with my soul still in the void. That's what they needed to do if they wanted a chance to rise again: keep my soul, no matter the cost.

Commanding the nio to seal off the entrance was a desperate move, but it was also their best option. Then they could do whatever they needed to keep me at arm's length while they used my soul to power their resurrection.

Of course, that had changed as soon as I pulled out the Lance of Longinus out of ... well, out of me. Of course, by then Jean had already made his way into the museum and, well, things went belly up from there.

But Jean and Keiko didn't know about the spear. From their perspective, the nio were doing them a favor by blocking the entrance. After all, that had been our original plan: lock the door, keep the bad gods inside.

"Why did you come inside?" I said. "They were doing your work for you."

Keiko nodded in agreement. "That would have been my choice," she said. Her voice betrayed no emotion—just the cold, hard fact. "Your death in exchange for the lives of so many. But Jean insisted that such a sacrifice was unacceptable. He risked all to save you and ..." Her voice trailed off, like she was debating whether to tell me what had happened next.

I remained silent. Keiko didn't owe me anything at this point. I had chosen my soul—my happiness—over trapping the gods. Sure, that plan wouldn't have worked, but we didn't know that at the time.

At the time, I was operating under the assumption that locking the gate was the best we could do, and me going in anyway betrayed my own selfishness.

If Keiko wanted to tell me more, she'd have to do so without selfish me pushing her.

We traversed the island for several minutes until the noro priestess broke her silence. "You know, Benkei did everything in his power to prevent us from entering the museum, but as soon as you went inside, he stopped. Then, when the nio sought to destroy the entrance, again he did nothing. He only animated the second Jean's intention to save you became apparent."

"Humph." I thought back to the warrior monk. He really didn't want me to get in and had done everything he could to stop me. "Why do you think that is?"

"I do not know," she said, "but I suspect that uncovering his motivations will do much for helping us undo what is being done."

"Good," I said, lacing the word with as much sarcastic venom as I could muster, "more mysteries to solve."

"More mysteries to solve," Keiko agreed with resignation.

↔

We marched forward until dusk, when finally we came upon a narrow path barely wide enough for us to walk on. The path led up the side of a rocky hill before we came upon a gateway where two old noro priestesses sat.

If either were troubled by the appearance of strangers, they made no show of it, smiling at us as we crossed under the threshold of the stone gates. We might as well have stepped through a time portal, because the village that met us didn't belong in a world with airplanes, cars and smart phones.

Hell, it didn't even belong in a world with steam engines.

We stepped onto a cobblestone road that led to a courtyard

surrounded by old stone cabins with thatched roofs. From the activities going on up ahead, it was obvious that the courtyard served as the village's heart, where everyone flowed in and out as they brought in crops and other goods necessary to sustain life.

The courtyard itself had a smart marketplace that, from the way the vegetables, fruits, fish and fresh cuts of meat were displayed, required no money to purchase the goods. The foods were there for anyone to pick up as needed. And from the amounts still sitting on the tables, it was clear that the people here only took what was needed and no more.

Also in the courtyard was a small clearing with a blackboard and chalk (probably the most modern amenities in the whole place). It looked like a small school where children and the newly mortal Others would be taught about the world they lived in.

Quaint, efficient, welcoming. This village was everything a community needed to survive.

But it wasn't what was here that made this place feel ancient—it was what was missing. There were pipes and wires to govern the flow of water and power, but there was no soft hum or drone echoing in the background. Nothing was illuminated by the false hues of man-made light. And nothing was branded with the marks of commercialism or ownership.

I stood in awe as memories of my own village flooded my being. It had been centuries since I'd seen a place like this, and given the way the world was going, I would never see anything like this again.

"Here," Keiko said, welcoming us into a large courtyard, "is where I was raised."

She guided us to the main building standing opposite of where we had entered, and if I had been worried that we would be showing disrespect to a culture and community older than any existing organized religion, that fear was short-lived ...

... and replaced by blinding fury. This peaceful village that had served as home to the priestess class for thousands of years was overrun by soldiers.

9

HOME NO MORE

*A*pparently we'd taken the back-door entrance, because as soon as we walked into the main courtyard, we were affronted by the hustle and bustle of activity.

Human soldiers flooded the village, forcing human and Other refugees alike from their homes and down the path toward the seafront. From the village's hilltop vantage point, I could see several boats waiting for their unwilling passengers.

And they weren't being nice about it, pushing the women down with apathetic vigor as they made them leave their homes. Homes, might I add, that they were planning to bomb the hell out of in a few hours.

I'm sure that in these guys' minds, they were saving lives. That they were taking these people away from the mounting army of hostile Others who lurked nearby, away from the island before the bombs started to drop.

But that's not how these women saw it; all they understood was that they'd lost their homes.

Now and forever.

A soldier pushed a young woman in a hurry-it-along gesture. The woman turned on her heel and kicked the grunt in the chin. He went down with a yelp as his buddies laughed. Out of sheer malice or thinking that somehow he was saving face, he got up and lifted a fist in the direction of the rebellious woman.

I didn't know if he planned to hit her or just wave his balled-up hand in her face. Either way, I wasn't standing for it and before he could get any closer to her, I stepped forward and kicked him in the back of the knee.

He dropped down to one knee like he was proposing to her and before he could stand up, I put a heavy hand on his shoulder and squeezed as if I was digging for his collarbone. If you squeeze just right that spot hurts the most, and when he gave me a satisfying yelp, I knew I was pinching the right nerves.

"Apologize to her," I growled. "Now."

He twisted his head to get a look at who was talking and when he saw a five-foot-nothing girl with impossibly beautiful auburn hair (hey, I'm pretty and I know it), I'm sure he thought this was some kind of joke. He started to stand and I pushed down with my hand, kicking him in the back of his knee once more. That forced him down again.

"I know what you're thinking," I said. " 'Here's some dainty girl who got in a lucky shot.' That you outweigh me by fifty pounds and you're a good foot and a half taller. You think you can take me. Let me assure you, this is a miscalculation on your part. So do the smart thing and apologize to her. Right now."

I don't know if it was the venom in my words or fire in my eyes that scorched his will to resist, but he turned to the rebellious noro priestess and said, "I'm sorry."

"In Japanese," I said, squeezing his collarbone.

"Ahh, I don't speak Japanese."

"Then repeat after me. *Gomen nasai.*" I said each syllable slowly, deliberately, just to make sure an idiot like this guy got it.

"*Go men nasai,*" he said, mimicking my cadence.

"Good," I said, nodding to the woman and letting him go.

↔

Keiko stepped forward, grabbing her noro sister by the hand and reassuring her that this wasn't the end of their home. That she would do everything in her power to reverse what was happening this day.

And as she spoke, several soldiers stepped forward, looking to back up their chum in a throwdown with *moi*. "Good," I said to the advancing squad. "Five against one. I could use the exercise."

Keiko, leaving the young noro, took a step forward. "Oops, looks like your guys are going to—"

"Enough," Jean groaned, as if bored. Making sure that his sleeve stripes were in full view, he said, "Step down, soldiers—they're with me." Then he looked at me. "Hulk much?"

"You should thank them," I said as they walked away. "I redirected a good portion of my rage at you toward them."

"Ahh, I see. In that case: thank you, boys," he said with a patronizing wave.

With the soldiers gone, Keiko surveyed her home that was emptying of life. A single tear flowed down her cheek as she said, "Katto-san, I have something to show you."

She gestured me out of the courtyard into another part of the village.

"I'll just hang out here," Jean said, "keep the boys in line."

I followed Keiko through the courtyard and toward a cluster of homes in the more residential area of the village. She brought us to the doorstep of one of those homes, sliding the door open. "This one has already been vacated."

We took our shoes off as we stepped into the traditional Japanese home. Keiko led me through the hall, lit only by the afternoon sun, to a bedroom with a series of tatami mats spread across it.

"This is where the priestesses-in-training sleep," Keiko said as we stepped into the room. She waved her arm around the space. "This is where my grandmother grew up."

59

I stepped through the doorway, my gaze sliding across the tatami mats as though they were occupied. As though the young priestesses slept on them even now.

I turned to Keiko. "She was safe here."

Keiko nodded. "Yes, Katto-san. As safe as a girl could be."

I had suspected as much, but hearing Keiko confirm it—and standing in this room where Blue had grown up—filled me with relief.

And even though she wasn't here, and hadn't been here for decades, something about knowing that Blue had spent years and years of her life here reminded me of my own humanness.

It reminded me that everyone who lived here right now was at risk of losing their homes, their history, their lives.

And I might be able to stop that from happening.

I turned to Keiko, bowed deeply. "Thank you."

She returned the bow. "After all this, I will take you to see her, if you like."

I smiled faintly. "Yes," I said. I wanted to carry the promise of seeing her again, even if I wasn't likely to leave this island alive. "I would like that."

↔

When we came back into the courtyard, Keiko left my side to talk to another noro priestess.

Ahead, Jean stood with his back to me, his arms folded as he watched the soldiers evacuating the village. I stepped up beside him, my gaze following his. "No more shoving the locals?" I asked.

"Not after your display," Jean said, chuckling. "I think they're more afraid of you than they are of me."

Good; I didn't want to have to send any more soldiers to their knees today.

Keiko approached us. "My sister has informed me that the soldiers are moving the Others last and that Father Time is still in his hut. This way," she said, and she led us up a path away from the village and into the mountainside.

10

KAT, MEET FATHER TIME FOR THE FIRST TIME

FATHER TIME, MEET KAT ... AGAIN

We trekked up the path where stone slabs had been built into the hillside as stairs, and from the overgrowth, I could tell that few people walked up here. Or down. Fresh prints from the soldiers' boots muddied the moss-covered stairs, and from the way the tracks appeared, three sets of boots had gone up slowly and then hurried down at breakneck speed.

Father Time is scary, I mused to myself.

"Father Time is not scary—just eccentric. The soldiers would not have run away from him," Keiko said, evidently listening in on my thoughts (the only explanation, because I'm pretty sure I'd nipped my "talk out loud" habit in the bud). We walked the last of the steps as she spoke, the stairs leveling out onto a plateau where two huts sat. Keiko pointed to the left hut. "Father Time lives there. It is the one who lives in the adjacent hut that they ran from. Come."

She gestured for us to walk to the left hut, standing in such a way that she blocked the path to the other home. Both Jean and I looked into the other hut's window as we walked, trying to get a sense of who lived there. We saw nothing, but that didn't stop the hairs on the back of my neck from standing at full, terrified attention. I'd been alive long enough—well, vampire-alive, which counts!—to know what I sensed.

A hunter.

And from the way every one of my senses screamed for me to run, that was one hell of a hunter.

"Who ... who lives there?"

Keiko shook her head. "That is not part of my compromise. I will not expose another to your musings."

Jean audibly gulped. Evidently he felt the same thing. "So we won't be speaking to the he, she or it who lives in there?"

Keiko nodded.

"Good," he said. "That's really good."

↔

Keiko lifted a hand to knock on the hut's entrance and as she made to rap on the wooden door, it swung open and her fist flew through empty air.

An old man with a long beard that wrapped around his ankles stood at the threshold. At least, that's what it looked like at first, but as he took a step into the light, I saw that the beard didn't just go straight down to his feet, but rather large tufts of it ran over his arms, stomach and around his back. He was literally clothed in his own white beard that covered him in a furry exterior that made him look like a white-furred yeti.

Harry would love this guy, I thought.

Father Time made a *come along* gesture as he stepped away from the threshold. "You two may enter. The noro may not. She has broken her oath to me and therefore she is one I can no longer speak to."

Keiko grimaced in visible pain at the words, but there was no surprise there. Others take oaths very seriously and when an oath is broken, their response tends to be harsh, final and often fatal. It was a small miracle that this guy didn't do more than simply shun her. In the grand scheme of Other logic, he was well within his rights to demand reparations that come in all sorts of nasty ways.

"Hurry along," he said. "I don't have all the time in the world to wait for you. Look at me … Father Time is running out of time." He giggled at his joke. Then his voice took an unnatural turn from jovial to deadly serious. "Hurry along. I don't have all day to reject you."

"Cheery," I muttered as I followed him inside.

↔

The inside of the hut was sparse, with one simple, single bed, one pillow and no sheets. Although it was small, the sparse furnishing made it roomy enough that the three of us could stand far enough apart to swing our arms without touching each other.

A single chair and table sat at the far end of the wall. Father Time gestured for me to sit on the chair. I was about to decline, but he said, "Yeah, yeah … you won't sit because you think I'm old and therefore my age and fragility trump your femininity when determining who is worthy of the chair."

Looking at Jean, he added, "And your youth and maleness preclude you from being offered the chair. Or at least, that is my understanding of human culture. Chairs are offered in the following order: pregnant, old woman, old man, child, young woman. Then there are the injured and handicapped to consider. If they are sufficiently hindered, then they go above all, even a pregnant woman near bursting. There are no offerings to a young man, unless said man is exhausted. Did I get that right?"

He waved a hand before either of us could answer. "Being mortal is so confusing. I guess that is what death gives us: a simplification of everything. Personally, I can't wait to be free of human protocol." He lifted his head up as if speaking to the wind. "Death, wherever you are, come and get me. I'm waiting."

Then he stopped speaking and looked at me expectantly. When I didn't say anything, he said, "Well, on with it."

"Ahh, OK," I said. "We have a … situation. Seems that three dead gods are seeking resurrection and the—"

"Yes, yes, yes. War, enslavement. Bombs, armies advancing. I've heard it all before," Father Time growled. "You know, we have met before."

"I don't think so," I said, searching my memories of the man. I had none. I mean, how could you forget a character like this guy? Even with clothes on, I would have remembered meeting him. "I think I'd remember meeting you."

Father Time looked at me with genuine confusion before shaking his head. "Ahh yes, you are right. I have met you before, but you have never met me."

"OK," I said, but before I could think of anything to say, Father Time started to laugh.

Then he abruptly stopped as if he was waiting for me to do or say something. Confused, I didn't move. "Go ahead," he said impatiently.

"Go ahead, what?" I said, turning to Jean for support. The soldier lifted his hands in surrender as he shook his head.

"Go ahead and make your joke."

"What joke?"

"The joke you're going to say. You know, I said, 'I have met you before. You have never met me, though.' To which you respond, 'That makes sense, and by makes sense, what I really mean is that doesn't make any sense at all.' Then I laugh." Father Time crossed his arms expectantly.

"OK," I said, unsure. "That makes sense, and by makes sense, what I really mean is that doesn't make any sense at all."

Father Time didn't laugh, but instead said, "I already chuckled at that one. Now impress me. Say something insightful."

"Insightful, eh?" I looked at a being that was literally responsible for the birth of time and tried to unpack what was going on in his impossibly old mind. He clearly wanted me to say something. No, that wasn't right—he wanted me to understand something. *"Say something insightful,"* he'd said, but just like he had laughed at a joke I hadn't said yet, he was waiting for me to say something that had already impressed him.

I thought about my eidetic memory. Most people who don't have it don't understand how such a memory works. They think we recall things, but we don't—not exactly. We recreate memories, remembering what happened by replaying the scene in our heads. And sometimes those memories can be so vivid it's as if we're reliving the moment again.

"You remember me," I said as my mind struggled to formulate the thought into something coherent, "because you can remember the future. You can remember things that have yet to happen, can't you?"

He snapped his fingers twice. "Precisely. You know, even though I remembered what you were going to say, I forgot how impressed I was going to be when you actually said it." He shook his head. "I guess my memory isn't what it once was. Comes from aging." Then he shot Jean a look and started to laugh.

Jean, taking the cue, said, "Ironic that Father Time is ravaged by time."

"Indeed!" he said. "You too are impressive, Mr. Jean-Luke Matthias, only missing the Mark."

Jean rolled his eyes. "I haven't heard that one before."

"I know, I know. And you will hear it many more times before you eventually find your Mark. But he's coming, that I promise you."

Jean lifted an eyebrow in curiosity. "What do you mean, 'find your Mark?' I—"

"Not now, Jean! We don't have time for this. Bombs are falling, gods are rising. We have work to do."

"So you're going to help us?"

Father Time shook his head. "No, I will not. I vowed when I became mortal that I would never lift a finger to guide the course of mortal affairs. And yes, I know that I am mortal. So no need to remind me," he said, looking at me. "And as for you, Jean, can we skip the part about how you don't really care, but you do love your wife Bella and you would do anything for her and how much she truly cares? And because you care for her, you in turn care for them—*us*." He added the last word as if it were an afterthought.

The old man stood up and pointed down the hill toward the village. "And I know you both will try to guilt me into helping by evoking memories of the priestesses' kindness and how this place creates a connection with the past and deserves a chance to remain. I will refuse you on all these counts and the dozen more arguments you will attempt to win me over with. So let's skip all that."

"Skip it?" I said. "Skip it! You can't be friggin' serious. You just had an entire conversation with us that we've never had … from memory. Your memory. A memory, might I add, that by your own admission isn't what it used to be. Perhaps there's a part of the conversation you've forgotten?"

"That may be," he said, "but even if you were to persuade me, I cannot help. I have sworn an oath to the departed gods never to intervene in the humans' course of time. That is why time travel is impossible. Time cannot be slowed, sped up or altered. And despite the prattling of numerous books and movies conjured by the human imagination, one cannot go forward or backward in time."

"Tell that to Marty and Doc," Jean muttered.

Father Time shot Jean a look and growled, "Time cannot be altered because of an oath I made before the gods brewed the primordial soup from which your ancestors emerged. I have not interfered with the mortal course of time since time began and I will not interfere now, even if it means that time may end."

"But the gods are gone—" I started.

"And I am not," he shot back. "I am here and intact. Ergo, my oaths are intact as well."

I was absolutely flabbergasted. To be rejected before we'd even gotten a chance to speak was devastating. If Jean was bothered by the whole thing, he didn't show it, simply shrugging. "OK, that's it. We'll be on our way then."

Father Time didn't say anything, but he did look at us expectantly, as if waiting for us to say something else. Something he remembered us saying. But it was more than his expectations that grabbed me. I also sensed a hint of fear in him.

Fear is a powerful motivator. It changes perspective, alters goals and ambitions, forces people to do things they'd never dream of. Things like breaking oaths.

He wants to help us, I thought as I considered Other logic. *He just needs us to force him into it.* But how do you force someone as ancient and powerful as the embodiment of time?

Not by threats or pleas, but with loopholes. Loopholes in the laws of the divine. And I had just the one.

"But here's the thing," I said, choosing my words with care. "How can you remember a conversation that is yet to happen? Also, riddle me this, Father Time: what will happen to you if we don't have the conversation? I mean, you just remembered something that hasn't happened yet. Surely not having the conversation will cripple you, won't it?"

Father Time considered this. Then his eyes widened. "I completely forgot this part. And yes, you're right—to not have this conversation would be akin to having a memory ripped from my mind. Very bad for the mortal condition. Not sure what would happen, but I hypothesize that to lose a memory in such a manner would bring on early-onset insanity." He shook his head as his lips trembled with fear. "I'm too young to go insane."

"And what would happen if you went insane? Certainly Father Time losing his mind would be detrimental to the very fabric of reality."

The old man considered this. "Perhaps I would do something horrible," he mused, "like alter the flow of time."

"Go back to before the gods left, for example?"

"Perhaps. Yes. Possibly. Probably." His eyes widened again. "Definitely."

"And that would be interfering with the mortal flow of time?" I said.

"Indeed. I would be breaking my oath."

"Then help us," I said.

"No. That, too, would be breaking my oath. You must plead with me and go through all the reasons for me to help you so that I may reject you."

"No," I said, folding my arms across my chest.

Father Time looked at Jean with pleading eyes.

Jean, seeing my plan, folded his arms before nodding in my direction. "What she said."

"But, but …"

"There must be a way you can help us without breaking your oath."

Father Time considered this. "There is a way, but it would be too close to the edge of the perimeters of my oath. Too, too close."

"Close only counts in horseshoes and hand grenades … and Black-jack," Jean said.

Both Father Time and I shot Jean an undignified look.

"Well, it's true," he muttered to himself like a sulking child.

Ignoring Jean, I said, "It's better to be close to the line and *not* cross it than cross the line, is it not? Help us and we'll help you. We'll have the conversation."

"But, but …" he stammered.

"You know the deal. Surely at this point you remember it, don't you? You know how this whole thing is going to unfold. Help us and we'll help you."

Father Time began clicking his tongue like the seconds on an old grandfather clock before nodding. "Very well," he said with a smile. "You have tricked me, placing me in a bind that forces my hand in order to maintain my vow. I shall help you. But not by shifting the sands of time. I shall instead impart a great secret to you that may, perhaps, if properly used, help you."

Then the creature who even the gods feared wrote something down on a piece of paper and folded it. Father Time handed it to Jean. "Open this when the time comes."

Jean started to protest, but he lifted a silencing finger. "And you will know when that time is. Trust me." Then he handed an ordinary hourglass in a wooden frame to me. It looked like a kitchen egg timer. "The sands of time, my young lady. Use them wisely." And with that, Father Time folded his arms. "Now let us have our conversation once more. And this time with feeling."

11
NO TIME LIKE ANY TIME BUT THE PRESENT

*W*e had our conversation. As for having it with feeling, I had to admit that even I was surprised by that part. And I'm not referring to what I said, because I was rather robotic in my role.

But Jean was another story. Sure, he started out robotic enough, just going through the motions, but as soon as he started talking about his wife, Bella, everything changed. He spoke about his love for her, her love for him … and how she had a heart so big that it loved everyone. And the more he spoke, the more we could feel his passion. He wasn't kidding when he said he loved her and would do anything to make her happy. To keep her safe. To help her on her mission to help Others. Jean might not have cared for Others in the way his wife did, but he cared enough for her that it spilled over into caring for them as well.

We stepped outside Father Time's hut. I held the hourglass, and Jean had the piece of folded paper that supposedly had something written on it that would help that would supposedly help us defeat the gods.

If this was "Mission Accomplished," then I'd hate to have gone through the mission-crashed-and-burned scenario.

Keiko, who had been sitting on a rock outside the hut, stood up as soon as we came out. She gave us a look that simultaneously prayed for hope mixed with a resolve that we'd go on even if there was none. How she managed to say all that with a look, I'll never know, but there was no denying Blue's presence in her granddaughter. If Keiko was half of who Blue was, she'd be a force to be reckoned with.

I gestured for us to walk down the path before saying anything. Once we were halfway down, Jean broke the silence with, "Well, that was special. I mean, I've met eccentric Others before, but this guy wins the beauty pageant for weird."

"I don't know," I said, "he was just working with what he had. He's an Other who used to live in all times at once. And now that he's mortal and stuck on the same temporal timeline as everyone else … well, it's a miracle he's not insane."

"You call that 'not insane?' " Jean said, cocking a thumb up the path.

"I call that surprisingly coherent. You saw what he did. He wanted to help us while not compromising his oaths. That's a big deal for normal Others, so I can only imagine how epically huge a deal it is for a creature with cosmic powers. But he played the conversation exactly how he needed to to get us to threaten him and—"

"You threatened him?" Keiko said, anger in her voice.

I waved a dismissive hand. "Yeah, but only because he wanted us to." And I told the noro priestess everything that had happened in the hut, ending with the folded paper and hourglass. "We don't know what this says or what the hourglass does, but he insisted we would know when the time comes."

"Does this mean he's seen the future and knows our outcome?" Keiko asked.

I considered this. Truth was, I had no idea.

Jean shook his head. "I don't think so. The way he spoke, the things he said, I gathered that the future isn't set and that there are many outcomes."

"But he is trying to help us?"

Again Jean shook his head. "He says he is, but I'm not so sure. A creature like Father Time would have a lot to gain from the gods returning. He'd be elevated to his previous status, become immortal again."

"True," I said, "but he'd also be enslaved by three gods whose Other-rights record wasn't exactly stellar. He didn't strike me as being into that, either."

Jean shrugged. "All I'm saying is that we take this vial of sand with a grain of salt." He chuckled at his joke. We did not. "Like I said," Jean chimed in after our groans, "I'm very funny in Paradise Lot."

Keiko pursed her lips, suppressing a … a smile. She wasn't actually starting to appreciate his jokes, was she? Then again, he did have a certain charm. *So does the Devil,* I thought, pulling my gaze away from him.

"OK," Keiko said, "so we have something with unknown powers that may or may not help us. I call that progress."

"Optimistic," I said.

"Perhaps, but it is something when before we had nothing. The question is, what next?"

"Well," Jean said, pointing down the hill at the destroyer floating off the coast, "we could jump on that ship and use all the gadgets they have to assess our next move. After all, knowing is half the battle."

G.I. Joe quotes aside, he was right. That ship would have access to information we didn't have, and right now we needed to know as much as possible if we were going to survive what was to come next.

End of Part 2

PART III
INTERMISSION

12

CHARON

ARRIVETH THE FERRYMAN

*C*haron lands on an island called Okinawa, a place he has visited many times before as the Ferryman. This is the first time he has traveled here as a mortal and he does not appreciate the long lines that he must suffer until he is granted final access to this place.

His attention is drawn to a young mortal talking to a giant yeti. They stand ahead of him, engaging in what the humans refer to as "pleasantries."

He does not know why his eyes fixate on her. She is young, virile, strong. Unless tragedy strikes, she will live for many more years. His desire for her is perplexing.

Charon is not attracted to the living; he only has eyes for the dead. And this girl is anything but …

He wonders what it is about her and considers exploring further. But before he can approach her, she is through the line and lost in the crowd of the Okinawan airport.

↔

. . .

Alone, lost and unsure of where to go next, Charon allows himself to be drawn toward the wayward soul. He finds himself standing on a port where many boats are docked.

He stares out toward the sea. His eyes—if you can call the all-seeing orbs that rest in his skull "eyes"—see another island across the sea. He knows that the soul isn't there.

Not yet, at least.

Wishing he had his ferry, he looks for a way across the waters and onto that island. And whether it's fate or destiny or inexplicable luck, his desire finds an answer in the yeti he saw speaking to that girl.

For the yeti recognizes him and says, "Charon, as I live and breathe! I had heard you were made mortal like the rest of us and had always hoped to meet you." The yeti extends a hand in a very human way.

Charon, as trained by Larry, takes the yeti's hand, much to the hairy beast's satisfaction. "Are you attending the festivities at Kakusareta Taiyo Shima? The Celestial Solace is tomorrow and we are headed there now."

The yeti points to a boat filled with other Others.

So that is where the soul is, Charon thinks. *Trapped in another plane of existence, waiting to come to this world so that it may find its living body once more.*

Charon nods, pulling out two pennies that he hands to the yeti as payment for passage.

The yeti accepts, holding the copper coins with the reverence befitting a gift from Charon the Ferryman.

↔

On the island, they walk to a familiar place: a hotel that Charon has visited many times while ushering souls to their various destinations. Once, he even escorted the god Baldr from the hotel to Yomi, the Land of the Dead and the geographical (well, celestial) location of the museum.

At the hotel, he sees many Others gathering for the coming Celestial Solace. The Land of the Dead is arriving this evening and all his senses tell him that the lost soul he seeks is trapped there.

This should be an easy affair, presuming that the pathways to the celestial plane will open up. Charon isn't sure what will happen now that the gods are gone.

But what makes him uneasy isn't the question of whether or not the pathway will open. It is the gathering occupants who line the halls of this place.

The Celestial Solace Hotel that Charon remembers is a place of peace. A place of neutrality. A place of reverence.

But the hostility within these halls is palpable. And Charon, who knows Death better than most, knows she will visit this place to reap the souls of many a lost Other.

His instincts are proven correct for at the moment when the human New Year and the Celestial Solstice intersects, a giant hole opens in the earth. It is not a pathway exactly, but more like a sinkhole into the underground passages that ultimately lead to Kami Subete Hakubutsukan and the museum beyond.

But as soon as the hole appears, the gathering Others engage in battle. For some reason, the battle seems to be centered around a young human. Charon cannot see the human and does not understand why the Others are so determined to capture her.

Then she jumps on the Chandelier of Stars and he sees that she possesses a map to Kami Subete Hakubutsukan.

He also sees that she is the one whose soul is trapped in the lands beyond.

13

G.I. JOE ... A REAL OTHER HERO!

*E*very time I thought I understood who this Jean guy was, he surprised me. Well, in this case, it wasn't that *he* surprised me —it was more the way everyone acted around him. The three of us had walked down to the shore where an obviously bored soldier stood counting the noro as they filed onto the ships. As soon as he saw Jean, his disinterest evaporated as he stood erect, his posture so perfect I thought his spine might fuse that way.

"Sir," he said, "so good of you to join us."

The other soldiers hadn't recognized him like this one did, and just as I was about to question how and why, I saw a little badge on his lapel with the initials OAIU. So he was from the same unit as Jean.

And from the way he swooned, I was starting to see that Jean wasn't just a high-ranking soldier in the OAIU ... he was a legend.

Jean gave the kid a half-hearted salute and a warm smile. "At ease," he said. Scanning the ships dotting the horizon, he pointed at the destroyer. "How do I get on that rust bucket?"

"The USS LaSalle?" the soldier asked. "We can chopper you in or speedboat or—"

"This isn't a multiple-choice quiz," Jean said with a wink. "I just want the quickest way on."

The soldier took Jean's wink like Deirdre might have taken a wink from Ryan Reynolds, because his knees went weak as a smile crept across his face that said, *"Wait until I get home and tell everyone what the great Jean-Luc Matthias did at me."*

Fanboy much?

"Speedboat," the soldier said, his tone relaxing. "The chopper will take time to arrange."

"Then a speedboat it is. Radio it in," Jean said.

The kid did more than radio it in. He went running to the beach-line, clicking his radio and waving his arms, and within sixty seconds, he was frantically calling us over to where a small, two-engine boat waited to speed us to the battleship.

"What did you do to get that guy's head stuck in your ass?" I asked.

"Nothing I'm proud of," he said with a solemn gaze.

↔

On the USS LaSalle, Jean, Keiko and I were greeted by the same bald captain that had sent us on our way when we'd sped off from Camp Kaneda and to this island. Only this time he had swapped his pristine white shirt with lots of medals and badges for a pristine blue blazer with lots of medals and badges and stripes.

Still, seeing the familiar captain gave me hope that Deirdre and Egya would be here to greet us as well. But a quick scan quickly revealed no changeling and no Ghanaian. *Military intelligence my ass*, I thought. *These guys have no idea what kind of assets they've been benching for this apocalyptic fight.*

"Actually, they know what kind of asset you are. They're holding the other two for insurance," Jean said, his hands up in a don't-shoot-the-messenger gesture. Jean turned to the captain, to whom he gave his characteristic half-salute. "Captain Donnelly."

The captain sneered at the obviously lax military protocol, but said nothing. Instead, he gestured for us to follow him into the bowels of the destroyer where we walked into a room with a low ceiling and lots of screens blipping and blooping. I felt like I had just entered the helm of a cliché submarine you saw in just about every 1980's movie.

All we need now is Sean Connery and we'll be in a scene from Hunt for Red October, I thought.

"Indeed, Moneypenny. Indeed," Jean said in a terrible Scottish accent.

"Stay out of my head," I said.

"Keep your head to yourself," he countered. And with a faux gentleman's bow, gestured for Keiko and me to take a seat.

The captain cleared his throat. Picking up a remote control, he activated a screen in front of the half-circle desk we sat on. "Here is the mystical hotel you called in. And as you can see, we've got one hell of an army gathering." He clicked twice and we saw the same scene that we had witnessed on Jean's tricorder device. The only difference was that the density of Others had grown.

As in, multiplied.

"And that's not the worst of it. Here." He clicked the remote twice and the screen's camera zoomed out and panned to the other side of the island before zooming in again. There we saw several aquatic Others—meres, hafgufa, umi zato and selkies—ferrying the non-swimming Others to the island.

"More and more are coming every hour. By tomorrow morning, the number of Others on the island should double, if not triple."

"And they're all gathering to protect the hotel?" I asked.

"That is our assessment—"

"No," Keiko said. "Look over there." She pointed to the upper right-hand corner of the screen. "Look—that is the makara who helped us to the island."

"Meres Griffin," Jean chimed in with a smile.

Without a hint of mirth, Keiko nodded in agreement. "*Hai.* The makara is against the coming of the gods. She does not wish for a new age of divinity. She fights against it."

Captain Donnelly pursed his lips as he considered Keiko's

comment. Then he walked over to a desk and pulled out some pictures. "Surveillance from this morning. There seems to be another camp of Others about two clicks from the hotel. And this morning, Others from that camp got into a skirmish with Others who had moved out from the hotel. We assumed it was just in-fighting. You know, one clan fighting for the top-dog position."

He tossed the pictures across the desk, which were full-HD images of dozens of Others engaging in a battle. As I pieced through them one by one, I saw several dead Others left behind on the field. Whatever this "skirmish" was about, it had claimed lives on both sides.

"So your theory that there are two forces pans out," the captain said with an even tone that betrayed the simple fact that, in his world, two opposing forces changed nothing. Especially if both sides were made of Others.

But just in case, I thought I'd drive it home. "You can't go ahead with the bombings—you'll be killing Others that are on the humans' side. On *your* side. Killing them will only galvanize the Others who are neutral against you."

The captain shook his head. "The boys in lab coats disagree. They think any decisive strike against an organized group of Others will serve as a lesson against organized rebellion. In fact, they theorize—"

"Then those lab-coat boys are stupid," I said. "As is your bombing raid plan."

"How do you figure, ma'am?" he asked, his demeanor not changing in the least. This guy was a career politician, which meant he was practiced at deflecting civilian objections to war.

"Well, for one thing," I said, raising a finger, "Others operate by a code of honor not too dissimilar to ours. You know, the whole Eye for an Eye thing. Except with these guys, they tend to go by Eye for Your Intestines."

The captain started to say something, but I shot him down by raising a second finger. "And for another thing, has bombing allies or innocents ever *not* resulted in radicalizing otherwise peaceful individuals?"

The captain shrugged. "That is a philosophical debate several rungs above my pay grade. We will continue as planned."

"And if you do," I said, slamming my fist on the table, "you will pave the way for the gods' resurrection. And that will lead to enslavement, torture, pain and suffering for Others and humans alike."

I took a deep breath, centering myself before I continued. "We have a real chance at stopping this," I said. "And bombing the island isn't necessary."

Captain Donnelly tilted his head in obvious confusion. "Yes, I got Jean's report and I must admit I found it all a bit odd. I thought the gods were gone?" the captain asked, and from his tone, I could tell he wasn't entirely sure what "the gods are gone" meant. For all he knew, a few of them had stuck around. Hell, for most humans, powerful Others were gods in their own right.

"The gods are gone," Jean said, "but apparently they didn't take their dead with them."

"Humph ..." The captain rubbed a thumb against his cleanly shaven cheek, an obvious nervous tic of his (may the GoneGods help him if he ever played poker). "I'm no doctor, but given that—according to you—they engaged in a conversation with you, these dead gods aren't really dead."

"There's dead and then there's *dead,* dead," I said, knowing that I was giving him the same kinds of cryptic answers I so often got from my Other friends. It felt good to share the misery.

My not-really-an-answer answer didn't seem to perturb the captain, though. "So these not-dead, still-somehow-dead gods ... who are they?"

"Baldr, Quetzalcoatl and Izanami," I said. "Three dead gods from three different pantheons who are trying to make a comeback in a big way."

"And we're only talking about three, right?"

I stared up at the tall captain. His uniform was immaculate, every nook and cranny ironed, his suit so pristine that he looked like older version of a Ken doll that had just been taken out of the box.

And from the ridiculous question Donnelly had just asked, it was obvious this guy knew nothing. It wasn't that he hadn't heard of these gods that made him ridiculous … it was that he was so obviously trying to wrap his head around the concept of magic and myths, resurrection and Others.

Given he was the guy the human world had sent to deal with the threat, I shouldn't have had to lecture him on stuff from Others 101.

"First off," I said, my voice dripping with disdain, "how many dead gods do you think there are? I mean, gods didn't go around slaying each other. And despite what Kratos did in the *God of War* video game series, mortals really didn't have the kind of power necessary to take down a god. So given the rarity of a god's death, do you really think there would be more? I mean, you're the guy in charge of fighting Others, because—what? You're qualified? I thought you actually had to know something to be qualified."

The captain's face turned beet red. He had just opened his mouth like he was going to start yelling when Jean chuckled. "She has a point. I mean, Captain, sir, she has a point, sir. Captain." He gave the befuddled commander a half-hearted salute.

The captain shot him a look that had probably sent hundreds of grunts running. Not that Jean seemed to care; he just looked back at the guy with disinterest.

Apparently, the seasoned military man had been in enough pissing contests to know when he should cut his losses. He took a deep breath, picked up his hat and tucked it under his arm before turning on his heel and heading toward the door.

"We start the bombing as soon as everything is prepped," he said.

"No—you can't! You have to give us more time," I said.

"I have to agree with her," Jean said. "A preemptive attack now may only serve to exacerbate the situation."

The captain pinched the bridge of his nose. "I have my orders. What do you suggest?"

Jean stood. "Your orders are what? To bomb the island? To wipe out the Other army, right?"

The captain nodded.

"And what about the timeframe?"

The captain didn't answer.

"No timeframe. Just an order to get it done, right?"

The captain was silent.

"Right?" Jean said, his tone commanding.

The captain nodded.

"Then here's my promise to you: you'll get to bomb the hell out of the island and you'll get your decisive victory. Just not yet. Give us a bit of time to launch an assault and save you money by identifying a surgical strike that doesn't take down our allies as well. You'll get your medals and the world won't descend into World War III. What do you say?"

I stared at Jean. Between "launching assaults" and "surgical strikes," he did a pretty good imitation of a man *not* pulling a plan out of thin air. When I looked back at Captain Donnelly, I just nodded solemnly as though Jean and Keiko and I had talked this all through beforehand.

Captain Donnelly considered this. From his body language, I was sure he was going to turn us down. As he went into deep thought, he touched a spot along the centerline of his jacket—a spot directly under his chin and low enough that I knew he wasn't subconsciously fiddling with something under his shirt. It was a pendant. And from the way his fingers moved, I guessed it was a cross.

The gods' departure had thrown faith—and, by extension, the faithful—into disarray. On the one hand, it had confirmed that the gods and capital *G* God existed. But on the other hand, they had abandoned us. What was the point in worshipping something we knew wasn't there?

Still, faith may have left us, but its guiding tenets hadn't. Some held onto those with furious fervor. Some, like this captain, weighed the cost of life against his orders. He was weighing the chances of peace against the chances of victory through destruction.

He pursed his lips before nodding. "Amendment to your proposal, soldier. I watch the hell out of the island and if I see any of them leaving, I rain holy hell on the place with everything we've got. If all is silent, then we follow your plan until dawn."

"Dawn?" I said.

"Dawn is the cut-off point. The bombs drop then, no matter what."

"But—" I started, but Jean lifted a silencing hand. He gave me a look that said, *"Don't push it, because this deal won't get any sweeter."*

Then Jean saluted Captain Donnelly—properly—and said, "Thank you, Captain."

"Yes, thank you," Keiko and I chimed in.

He grunted. "I'm not doing this as a favor to any of you. I'm doing this because, strategically, it makes the most sense. Now, if you don't mind." He tucked his hat under his arm as he turned on his heel and headed for the door.

And with that, he left Jean, Keiko and me in the metal tomb of this battleship's bowels.

"That went well," Jean said.

I shrugged. "I don't really care how it went. We've got to figure out how to stop these guys."

"Agreed," Jean said, before scratching his head. "So how do we do that?"

Yep—my whole "pulling a plan out of thin air" theory about everything Jean had just spouted off to Donnelly had been 100% correct.

We sat in silence for a long minute before Keiko said, "Can I get to the water? I shall call the makara—"

"Meres Griffin," Jean chimed in.

"You're like a dog with a bone," I said. "Please Keiko, go on …"

She gave me a curt bow. "I shall call the makara and ask the great sea creature what is happening. Such information will be valuable to us."

"Agreed."

"Not so simple," Jean said. "These guys are trigger-happy. A giant sea creature shows up and they'd be all *pew pew*." He gestured with his pointer finger and thumb out as he made the laser gun sounds. "But we can get that grunt to speedboat you far enough away to avoid any friendly fire."

"Make it so," I said.

"*Star Trek* joke?" Jean asked.

I nodded.

"Because me and the captain of the Starship Enterprise share the same name?"

Again, I nodded.

"But I'm not the captain of any ship, Starship or otherwise. You know that, right?"

I gave him a blank look.

"Just to avoid any confusion: Jean-Luc Picard, him. Jean-Luc Matthias, me."

"Now you're trying to annoy me," I groaned.

He pointed at me. *"Pew pew."*

↔

Jean called it in, and within minutes Keiko was whisked away to have her little chat with Meres Griffin (hey, the name worked), leaving Jean and me alone in the USS Destroy Everything at Dawn.

"Now what?" Jean asked.

If we were back in Montreal, I would have suggested going to the Other Studies Library and hitting the books. But given we were on a ship on the other side of the planet, that wasn't really an option. Still, we weren't without resources. Or rather, we weren't without access to those with resources. "Does this floating bathtub have Wi-Fi?" I asked.

14
WHAT'S THE PLAN, PHIL?

*J*ean logged me into one of the terminals using his login details. The first scene that came up had three folders on it, which were labeled: Active Missions, Classified and Toys Yet To Be Purchased.

"Toys yet to be purchased, huh?" I said. "RPGs, semi-automatics … an iron maiden from Medieval Torture 'R' Us? You know, I was put in one of those and—"

Jean was clearly annoyed by me chiding him, because he clicked on the folder and said, "No, just toys." In the folder, images of He-Man, Cabbage Patch dolls, G.I. Joes, Transformers, Voltron and Smurfs appeared on the screen. His eyes lit up on seeing them. "That's what I've either collected or kept from my childhood. This folder is what I have left to collect and—"

"I get it," I said. "You're a geek."

"At your service, ma'am." He gave me a real salute instead of the half-hearted ones he'd given his superiors. Then he closed the folder with a mutter. "Simpler times. So what do you want?"

"Chrome."

"Chrome?"

"Or Firefox, Safari … any browser other than Explorer, really."

"You want access to the Internet? We literally have the greatest Other database ever conceived and you want ... what, Wikipedia?"

"Actually, Twitter for reliable sites and Reddit for knowledgeable people. I want to talk to some online peeps who actually know their history and mythology. Unlike Captain Crunch out there."

Jean clicked on an icon that brought up a screen typical of Windows 10 and clicked on the Chrome icon. "Here you go," he said. "And as for Captain Crunch, I give him a hard time, but he's one of the good guys."

"In my limited three hundred years of experience, I've come to learn two truths. One—the real bad guys are the ones who think they're the good guys."

"And," Jean said gesturing for me to hurry up with my point.

"Two," I said, drawing out the word for an unnecessarily long time ... you know, just to annoy the soldier, "good guys have to do bad things to stop them."

"Humph," Jean said. "Cynical much?"

"You would be, too, after what I've—"

"—seen?" Jean interrupted.

"Done," I corrected.

I clicked on the search bar and logged onto Twitter. "Let's start with our Norse god, shall we?" I muttered to myself and typed Baldr's name followed by #FolkloreThursday. Immediately several searches came up with his name. "Before the gods left, this was a pretty cool hashtag created by people who love mythology, legends, old stories. You know, the non-toy geeks."

"Hey, it's a Venn diagram," Jean said.

I nodded. "But after the gods did their whole GrandExodus thing, this hashtag exploded, with the diehards archiving everything known. And I have it on very good authority that there are some heavy-hitter Others that contribute to this every week."

"Like who?"

"Like Penemue and the Sphinx, to name a couple."

Jean ran his hand through his hair. "Holy guacamole. Penemue, I don't know, but the Sphinx? That's about as heavy-hitting as you can get knowledge-wise. How the hell does the army *not* know about this?"

I shrugged. "I have my theories and you wouldn't like any of them." I opened more browsers and repeated the search term for the other two dead gods.

The initial information that came up was fairly typical stuff, everything we already knew about the three dead gods. Baldr was killed by a spear made out of mistletoe; Izanami was trapped by her once husband Izanagi; Quetzalcoatl slept with his sister and, out of shame, killed himself on a funeral pyre made by his servants.

Like I said: typical stuff.

They all died, true, but each came from a pantheon with the power of resurrection. And their counterpart gods chose not to raise them from the dead. Izanami because it was feared that death had corrupted her. Baldr because they believed his death was a sign of Ragnarök. Only Quetzalcoatl's myth stories didn't give a reason for why he remained dead.

Deirdre had mentioned on the plane over to Japan that a deal had been made with the gods after Jesus's resurrection. No god could return any dead thing back to life, but that didn't explain why these dead gods weren't brought back. They had all died before Jesus— before the accords.

That gelled with what Aki the tanuki had said about the gods ... about how vile they were and more of a liability than anything else. But still, so many gods did so much shitty stuff that these guys' crimes fell pretty firmly in the bog-standard column of the Horrible Stuff Gods Do category.

"This is useless," I said. "We're not learning anything new."

Jean nodded. "I was hoping to find some commonality between the three, but I can't. You can find common elements between two of them easily enough, but all three?" He shook his head.

"OK, let's work on a dual basis. What do we get?"

"Quelzalcoatl and Baldr were both burned on a funeral pyre. Izanami and Quelzalcoatl both manifested something after their death. Quelzalcoatl manifested flocks of birds and Izanami created monsters called shikome after she died. Baldr and Izanami's pantheons both believed that their deaths were a sign or stepping stone toward the end of the world—"

"And all three were left behind when the apocalypse happened," I added.

"So? It wasn't like the gods leaving ended everything."

"True, but maybe that's out of design. Think about it: immortal beings don't exactly think in terms of immediacy. Maybe their leaving was step one. Step two is these guys return."

"So what? We're on the Seven Step Plan for the Apocalypse?"

I shrugged. "Maybe? Two out of three are signposts for the end of days. And as for the third one—Quelzalcoatl—he ... he ..." I snapped my fingers as I jolted back to the computer. "Where is it? Where is it?" I said as I went through my searches, looking for a tidbit of information I had bypassed. Finding it, I clicked on the link. "Here."

"The Book of Mormon?"

"Yeah." I smiled. "Our Venn diagram finally has a three-circle overlap."

"Again ... *The Book of Mormon*? Outside of scratchy underwear, what do the Mormons have to do with the end of days?"

"Read here," I said. " *'The story of the life of the Mexican divinity Quetzalcoatl closely resembles that of the Savior'* ... as in Jesus Christ."

"Yeah," Jean said, "but it also says that the theory was debunked as folklore."

"So? We live in a world that is literally one huge, world-shattering debunking of folklore. What if"—I looked at the name—"John Taylor the church leader is right? What if Quetzalcoatl is Jesus? Then his return is a sign of the Apocalypse."

"Our overlap," Jean said with a groan.

Normally figuring out something like this would have resulted in a victory lap, but all we really managed to uncover was that the three dead gods shared one common trait: their return meant the end of days.

↔

"OK," Jean said, "but we're still no closer to anything we didn't know already. All we've done is upgraded this from a gods-are-coming-to-enslave-us bad to a gods-are-coming-to-kill-us bad. We still don't have a plan other than that we need to stop them."

"Which is something I was doing until you pulled me out."

Jean waved a dismissive hand. "Spilled milk and all that."

I leaned back in my chair, rubbing my temples. I had no idea what we needed to do other than get me back into the Kami Subete Hakubutsukan, where I stood a fighting chance of taking them down. And all that was predicated on the hope that I could get the god-killing Lance of Longinus back and that the gods hadn't gathered enough power to be more of a challenge.

"If ever we needed a miracle, now's the time," I muttered. And as if answering my prayers, a radio crackled in the room.

↔

Keiko's voice came through the speakers. "Jean, Kat ... I have spoken to the makara."

I looked over at Jean, expecting him to repeat his joke, but the soldier didn't and I took it as a bad sign. He was giving up, and right now we needed all the fight we could muster.

"We're here and listening. Go on," Jean said.

"I have spoken to the makara," she repeated. "Explained our situation. They are willing to help us engage the enemy. A coordinated attack is to happen at midnight—this evening. They will help us find a way back into the museum."

That wasn't good enough.

"But the bombs will go flying at dawn," I said. "The last time I was in there, I was gone for thirty-six hours. We'll be caught in the explosions."

The radio didn't answer; only the crackling sound of wind and solemn contemplation came through.

For a long moment we didn't move, didn't say anything. Until finally the noro priestess's voice came through: "Three lives for the world. It is a small sacrifice."

Jean sighed. "Maybe not. We have no idea how the bombing will affect anyone actually inside the museum. We could all go inside and—"

"Potentially give the gods two more human souls to amp up their powers?"

"Yeah, but you were super-charged in there. Control the controllable ..." His voice trailed off as he went through the logic. "We don't really understand how this works, do we? But the dead gods do. We can't risk that. Control the controllable," he repeated.

"Fine," I said, "I go alone."

"No, Katto-san, you will not go alone."

Jean shook his head, too. "Can't let you do that. What we can do is get you in as soon as possible and then the noro and I beeline it to the shore in the hopes of missing the fireworks. The timing will be tight, but ..." From the way he spoke, I understood that he knew full well going on this mission was a suicide mission for him and Keiko. Probably for me, too.

But apparently in the Venn diagram's overlap of Keiko, Jean and me, we shared one undeniable, frustrating quality: we were all willing to die for what we believed was right.

15

NOT ALL GOODBYES ARE
CREATED THE SAME

*I*t's not every day that you get to prepare for a suicide mission.

I mean, I've gotten myself into situations where the chances of survival have been in the one- to three-percent range, but this was different. We were facing off against an army of powerful Others who didn't mind using magic because, by their estimation, when the gods returned so would unlimited access to their magic. We were up against a ridiculously tight timeframe because the non-magical humans were going to drop their bombs in five hours. And to top it all off, we were about to face three dead gods who were more powerful than ever.

So I put the chances of surviving this one at about a minus four percent. Granted, we had a couple cards up our sleeve: the note and hourglass from Father Time and some Others determined to defend their new home, but somehow I just didn't think that was enough.

This was the end. This was how it ended for me: with a boom. My only consolation was that if I did manage to stop the gods, then my death would be the only one.

It wouldn't be everyone's death. It wouldn't be Deirdre, or Egya, or Justin, or anyone else I loved.

My other consolation was that if I failed, then I wouldn't be dying alone. So all in all, a win-win.

We got on the speedboat and headed toward the Other army. As we cut through the water, Jean handed me a satellite phone. "Anyone you want to call?"

I thought about it. I could call Justin, but things were so strained between us that I knew speaking to him would only get into my head, and right now I needed to focus on what was happening.

So no Justin. That left my mom ... and she was the last person I wanted to talk to just before biting the big one. She'd probably tell me I was dying wrong. Then there were Egya and Deirdre. I would have loved to speak to them, but they were being held at Camp Kaneda, probably one of the safest places to be ... thank the GoneGods for small miracles.

I shook my head and Jean gave me a pitying look before saying, "You steer. I have someone I need to speak to." Then he dialed a number and after a couple seconds, I heard him say, "Hi, babe."

Jean moved to the front of the boat for some privacy, and with the wind blowing, he needed to put his back to the front of the boat, which meant he was facing me.

I couldn't hear a thing he was saying. But I could read lips. It was a skill I'd picked up during my hundreds of years of hunting.

I tried to look away, to give him his privacy. I knew it was the right thing to do, but the alternative was looking at the sea and contemplating my own death.

So, taking the high road, I eavesdropped (well, eye-dropped) on the last phone call he'd ever make to the love of his life.

"How's the hotel going?" he asked before chuckling at something she said. "Well, you tell Miral that she's an angelic pain in my wingless ass." He was smiling as he spoke. "And how's Judith? Not that I care how your ghost of a mother is doing. I only ask because I know that you like it when I do."

More chuckles before he said, "That's good." Then he paused before his lips pursed. "It's so good to hear your voice. It will always amaze me how everything becomes OK with just one word from you.

Yeah, I know it's windy. I'm on a boat, heading in for another mission. Dangerous? Isn't every mission?"

Jean ran his hands through his hair as he closed his eyes. "Bella, I'm sorry. Sorry I couldn't be the man you wanted me to be ..." He put up a hand. "No, hear me out, please. I'm sorry for not being the man you deserved. I wanted to be that guy—really, I did. Hell, all I ever wanted was to make you proud. You know, help the Others just like you do. I just want you to know that, in my own way, that's what I'm doing. Helping in the way I believe is best. I know that my job—me hunting some of them down—seems like I'm doing the opposite, but the way I see it is that we have to uproot the worst of them before humans will accept them as part of this world. I may be wrong, but that's what I'm trying to do."

A single tear escaped his closed eyes. "That's what I will continue to do until the day I die: help the best way I can and hope—pray that I'm making you proud." There was a long pause as she spoke words I couldn't hear. He was nodding. "Yeah, I know. I know. I love you, too. In this world and the next—I love you, too."

He wiped away the tear that had caught on his cheek. "Look, I got to go. You tell Miral good luck with her medical exams and tell your mom that I hope she's keeping well. Oh, and make sure when you deliver the message to your mom that your tone conveys the sincerity I feel in my heart."

There was another pause before he nodded and whispered, "In this world and the next." And with that he hung up.

The obvious pain on his face, the clear love he felt for his wife ... it was all too much, and I did something I hadn't done since I lost my soul. I cried.

Jean looked up at me and mouthed, "Lip reader."

I nodded, wiping away a tear.

"I should have known," he said with a shrug, before turning to face the horizon we were speeding toward.

16

WE MAKE PLANS AND THE GODS LAUGH

O ur speedboat met up with the larger vessel that held Keiko. Waving at the noro priestess, I noted that the water around us got very dark, but before I could see what was beneath us, Jean yelled out, "Meres!"

My body tensed as I prepared for another battle with the murderous and nothing-like-Daryl-Hannah-in-*Splash* creatures. Jean chuckled and added, "Griffin."

Walking to the front of the boat where a soldier extended a hand to help him onto the bigger vessel, he slapped me on the shoulder. "Lighten up, kid. If today we die, then let's do it with a smile."

"You remind me of Egya," I said, taking his hand as support to climb up onto the boat. "He's a pain in the ass, too."

↔

The soldiers manning the boat hopped onto the smaller speedboat and returned to the fleet. I guess suicide missions weren't in their job description. *Fair enough*, I thought. Then looking over at Jean, I wondered why they were in his.

I mean, I knew why they were in mine. I had enough bodies in my past to fill the entire cast of extras on *The Walking Dead*. And they followed me everywhere, demanding retribution. Dying while trying to save the world wouldn't change my debt to them, but it would go a fair distance toward unburdening my soul … if I ever got that back.

I also understood Keiko's reasons for being there that day. She was a noro priestess—the spiritual equivalent of a guardian. Taking up that mantle wasn't something you did lightly, and I knew that when she wore the white sash, she did so fully willing to sacrifice herself for the greater good.

But whatever Jean's reasons were for joining us so willingly, they weren't something I was going to ask him about. Not now, at least. I needed his help getting to the museum. *If*—and that was a very improbable, unlikely, never going to happen *if*—we survived, I'd ask him then.

I had to admit, my curiosity for his answer burned strong enough that I wanted us to survive.

But as we followed the makara toward their impromptu base of gathering Others and I saw just how many had shown up to fight against the resurrection of the Three Who Are One, I wondered why any of them were here.

↔

It was ten o'clock—as in, only a handful of hours until the bombs dropped—when Meres Griffin led us as close to shore as her massive body allowed.

A leshy riding a winged horse flew to greet us. "Welcome, Lady Noro." He wore a wooden club at his hip and looked like an ordinary —albeit quite tall—man, and I might have mistaken the leshy for one if it wasn't for his beard. The thick bush that ordained his face was made of living grass and vines twisting in the wind. "I am Lazlo, the undeserving leader of this ragtag gathering of noble heroes. We understand that you have come to lend your aid."

As he spoke he looked only at Keiko, like she was the only one on the boat.

The noro priestess met his gaze before answering, "*Hai*, that we are."

As soon as the word "we" came out of her mouth, the leshy acknowledged Jean and me. Not that I cared—I was too busy fangirling super hard over Pegasus. I just couldn't believe I was not only staring at the legendary winged horse, but also basking in the fanning of the legendary creature's wings. "Holy shit," I murmured. "As I live and breathe … Pegasus. Incredible."

"It is indeed, milady," said the leshy. He patted her on the neck. "This divine creature was instrumental to the slaying of a Titan. Her experience will be invaluable now that our sights are trained on a god." As he spoke, I noted that he might have been responding to my comment, but he only spoke to Keiko.

There were some power dynamics going on, which weren't lost on Keiko. Placing one hand on my shoulder and the other on Jean's, she said, "Indeed. As will the experiences and abilities of my two companions."

This seemed to placate Lazlo, who looked at me for the first time with a wicked smile that would have fit the lips of a fox. "Come. Follow us and let's deliberate, scheme and organize."

I nodded in approval, then stole another glance at the legendary winged horse. Seeing him filled me with hope that we might actually win the day. But instead of saying anything to that effect, I just muttered (more to myself), "I've really got to write Medusa a letter and let her know who I just met."

"Medusa, huh?" Jean said, lifting an eyebrow. "Not to name-drop or anything, but I've met the gorgon."

"You and me too, buddy," I said with all the bravado of a drunk in a pissing contest. "You and me too."

. . .

↔

The sun had long set when Lazlo led us to a marquee tent in the middle of a camp filled with just about every Other I could think of. Skeletal ahkiyyini, bright rainbow crows and thunderbirds, floating peris and weird, haglike kikimoras. Two hieracosphinxes flew above our heads, an aqrabuamelu sharpened the dart at the end of his scorpion's tail, a tu-te-wehiwehi croaked ballads about war and love, loss and victory. Hell, I had thought the party at the Celestial Hotel was filled with a who's who of Others, but it paled in comparison to this.

I guess nothing brings out the masses like war. The idea was so depressing to me that even though that particular thought was voiced only in my head, my brain made such an audible sigh that everyone looked at me.

"Sorry," I muttered as we walked through the war camp.

One of the oddest things about that short walk wasn't just the variety of Others present—it was that they all stared at us. At first, I figured that an army primarily comprised of mythical creatures didn't take kindly to us human folk (thought in a Southern accent garnered from the six months I spent biting rednecks in Alabama). But following the Others' eyes, I quickly realized that they weren't staring at *us*.

They were staring at Keiko. And not only staring, but awe-ing—as in eye-widening, jaw-dropping awe-ing. Noro had crazy street cred amongst the Others.

I'd had no idea.

But from the way Keiko held herself—the slight nods, the gentle gestures of acknowledgement—she knew full well what her status meant.

And from the determination in her walk, she knew exactly how she was going to use that influence. All I knew was that we wouldn't have been let onto the island without her and the only reason our entrails weren't decorating some ugallu's armor was because of her.

Well, because of me, and what I did several decades ago when I saved Blue, I thought. And even though I knew I had very little do with what was happening here, I did wonder if destiny had played a role in all this.

Think about it: over seventy years ago, I'd saved a little girl who, because of me, was adopted by noro priestesses. And now, seventy years later, her granddaughter was fighting by my side because of what had happened all that time ago.

The gods may be gone, but the mystical roads of destiny and fate still lingered on.

Then again, it could have been coincidence. But what was destiny other than prescribing meaning to the random events littering our universe?

We were escorted to the marquee—obviously somehow stolen from the hotel—where a storm giant stood guard at the threshold. The giant's eyes bristled with ice-blue electric currents. When a storm giant hit you, you didn't just feel the brunt of a powerful fist ... you were also struck with several thousand jolts of electricity. It was like getting hit by a defibrillator attached to a nuclear power plant.

Seeing all these powerful creatures in one place, I began to wonder if we had a chance after all, but then I remembered the satellite pictures. The *other* Other army was twice as large as this one, equally equipped with powerful Others and they had a flight of dragons hovering over the hotel.

Still, giants vs. dragons ... that would be one hell of a fight.

"Welcome," Lazlo said, pointing to the battle table in the center of the tent. It was quite literally a Warhammer tabletop, complete with figurines from the toy company's collection. "This layout is courtesy of our fairy scouts."

Jean pulled out satellite imagery from his backpack and compared the maps. While the military photographs showed the hotel encampment, the flight of dragons and the platoon of various Greek and Japanese creatures to the north, they did not show the three legions of

Others hidden in various parts of the forest that stood between this camp and the hotel.

"So much for military intelligence," I said, pointing to the groups.

Jean grunted.

"What are those?" Keiko asked.

"Ahh, these here are Mongolian death worms buried under the earth." He pointed to the cluster closest to the camp. "And as for the two other groups, they're both composed mostly of aboveground Others of various woodland occupations. Very adept at hiding, very deadly."

"And your fairy scouts found them."

"While a whowie is adept at camouflage and hiding, a fairy is good at finding," he said.

It was true: almost nothing could hide from a fairy and it was a common motif in myth to request a fairy's help in finding a lost artifact or person. But the trouble with fairies was that, while they were competent scouts, they had goldfish-like memories and were extremely easy to distract. The mere fact that fairies had created such a comprehensive map showed their commitment to the cause.

"Incredible," I said.

"No kidding," Jean agreed. "No kidding."

I pointed at the passageway by which Jean and I had originally entered the subterranean tunnels leading to the museum. Then, rolling up my sleeve, I looked at my map tattoo. It still showed about three inches of blank flesh between us and the red dot near my wrist that represented my soul. The only coloring was a single orange line that extended from the hotel down into the tunnels.

To get in, we'd need access to the hotel and that was the most heavily guarded part of their whole damn operation.

"Anything?" Keiko asked.

I shook my head. "We either need to get down the hole in the foyer of the Celestial Solace Hotel or find a creature that can tunnel its way through here and into the hotel. Don't suppose you have any ramidreju in your ranks?"

Lazlo shook his grass-covered head. "Terrible creatures—very greedy. No sense of nobility amongst the lot them."

"I don't know about that," Jean said absentmindedly as he walked around the table. "You just need to give them what they want. I mean, isn't that how we all work? Give us what we want and we'll do anything, right?" Jean looked up from the table and smiled. "And what do these guys want right now more than anything?"

Lazlo spat a moss-covered spitball onto the earth. "To be enslaved by an unworthy divinity."

"Exactly," Jean said. "Tell me, did your scouts confirm that they are actually at the Kami Subete Hakubutsukan entrance?"

Lazlo nodded.

"Are they entering?"

"Some have tried, but none have a legitimate claim and therefore are not allowed in."

This is interesting, I thought. I was able to enter because my soul was inside, but so was Jean. Why? It didn't make sense. His soul wasn't trapped inside. Hell, the only claim he had was to save my ass, and given that he'd just met me, that wasn't much of a claim. Cosmically speaking, that is.

The way Jean's eyebrows furled, I could tell he was thinking the same thing.

"So, riddle me this," Jean said. "They want the gods inside to rise. They are so desperate to make that happen that they've literally gathered an army to protect the entrance. And they still don't have a legitimate claim? And that's just to enter once. What the hell do you have to do to get a season pass?"

"I can answer that," Keiko said, stepping toward the map. "The noro have protected this place for centuries, using our influence to closely guard the secrets within. I know what is inside and my heart trembles with fear at the thought of it. When the gods created this place, they did so in such a way that power may come in and out."

"We know that already—"

Keiko raised a silencing hand. "But such power had to be trapped within its halls. Imagine what would happen if it were removed easily. The power in those halls could rival gods, so they designed a safety mechanism to keep the power within. But it is more than that."

"More than what?" Jean asked.

"Kami Subete Hakubutsukan is referred to as a gallery, but that is a quaint term for what it actually is. Make no mistake as to what it is: a prison. A prison for items of power and for creatures too evil to be allowed to exist and too powerful to kill. The Three Who Are One are but three creatures housed in those halls."

Keiko hadn't called Kami Subete Hakubutsukan a museum, but a "gallery." I thought about that word, and I remembered that gallery didn't always have the artsy, benevolent meaning it does now. Back in the day—my day and before—they used to call a zoo a gallery. And before then, prisons.

The noro eyed me as she spoke and I saw guilt painted on her face. She wasn't aiding me because once upon a time I had saved her grandmother, Blue. Nor was she helping me because I had a legitimate claim to my soul. She was playing another game altogether.

I thought about the lock she'd given me and how she had instructed me not to enter, but rather get to the threshold and lock the museum's doors forever. Her gamble was about preventing creatures with legitimate claims from entering. As in, ever.

"The gleipnir chain," I said. "It wasn't meant just to keep things out of the museum ... it was also meant to keep everything in."

She nodded.

So the noro had foreseen the danger of creatures like myself—creatures with legitimate claims—entering the museum and exiting with ... I don't know, how about immortality granted by the Golden Apple or Dionysus's thyrsus, an item so powerful it was said that a scratch from it would drive one insane? Or how about Jack's Lantern? As in, the actual lantern used by the first soul condemned to wander Earth. It was legend that its light could destroy shadows.

And I'd screwed it up by going all rogue and entering for my soul.

"Who else is inside?" Jean asked.

"The Erlking, Azazel and the Kraken, to name a few."

"Holy guacamole," I muttered. Of all the bad in the world, those were probably the top three on the Other Watch List.

Lazlo shook his head in disbelief. "All this time I thought it was but a place of magic only ..."

"That was by design," Keiko said. "Imagine if the elements of the UnSeelie Court who worshipped the Erlking knew their master lived. And what's more, that he was in the halls of Kami Subete Hakubut-sukan? The place would be under constant bombardment from wayward Others looking to free their masters."

"OK, but if that's the case, how did all these Others know about the rising of the gods?"

"The same way any god rising to power delivers their message: Heralds."

"Heralds?" Jean spat the word like it was sour milk. "You mean those blind dorks who always seem to show up with the nio guardians?"

Keiko nodded. "Heralds ... would-be prophets driven mad by the words that gods whisper into their ears. To most, they seem like raving lunatics, but to those who know—to Others who know—they are revered as what they truly are: prophets."

"And what was Gabriel's legitimate claim?" I asked. "He's inside, right? Why does he have the right to enter when no one else does?"

Keiko shook her head. "I do not know."

"OK, history lesson aside, we're still no closer to a plan."

"I think we are," Jean said. "I think we do the Queen Bee strategy."

We all looked at him blankly.

"What? Not Animal Planet fans? The Queen Bee strategy: when a colony is destroyed and they need to set up camp somewhere else, the bees swarm around the queen bee, protecting her at all cost, while moving her to a new location. In this analogy, you're the queen bee and this army, well ... you get the point."

"You realize that you just called me an insect whose sole purpose is reproduction."

"I called you a queen," he said. "But regardless, we launch an offensive here and cut through the center." He pointed to the section of the map with the Mongolian death worms. "I saw that there were several ijiraq in camp—they should be able to neutralize the worms. Once we're past this threat, we break off with two units playing linebacker defense and cut through here. There will be a lot of resistance, but once we make it to this point, we can use the confusion to break away. Just the two of us."

"How endearing," I said. "Will you hold my hand, too?"

"Cute, but pay attention." He set his finger to two points near the hotel. "If we can get to here undetected, I can get you in."

"How do you figure?"

He pulled out his tricorder. "Remember the tracker you left in the hole? It also has a sonar blip to it, for exactly this kind of infiltration." He showed me the screen where several caverns twisted beneath the earth, leading to the tracker. "This location should be close enough that your magical arm map will actually show something. This is our back door in, and once you're in, you do your soul magic stuff and bada bing, bada boom, we're done."

"In other words: get me back to where I was to finish the job," I said, jibbing at Jean's very chivalrous and completely unnecessary saving of *moi*.

"Again, sorry. And again, spilled milk. Lazlo, how long until your troops are ready?"

"We will be ready to attack at midnight."

"There you go. We have a plan," Jean said, looking at his Mickey Mouse wrist watch. "So in two hours …" He paused, and I saw him mouthing numbers to himself before his eyes widened. "Shit," he cried out. "Get down! Someone is burning time."

As the words left his mouth, a banshee manifested. The creature must have been invisible the whole time, listening in on our plans.

The banshee let a shriek that could have been heard on the moon. What followed were several more shrieks and explosions. The Others were attacking.

So much for our plan.

17

CRY "HAVOC!" AND LET SLIP THE OTHERS OF WAR

*W*ith lightning-fast reflexes, Jean pulled out his Ka-Bar and sliced open the banshee's throat. *GoneGodDamn*, I thought, *he's fast. Faster than I am now. Maybe even faster than I was as a vamp.* The banshee's screams abruptly stopped, the shrill, piercing noise replaced by the gurgling of green blood as she tried to continue her scream.

Jean may have been fast, but she had delivered her message and the advancing army had been poised for action. Immediately, explosions rang throughout the camp and as we ran out of the tent, a friggin' fireball exploded just feet from the entrance. Thank the GoneGods for my smallness, because had I been a couple inches taller, that lower crest of the ball would have singed my impeccably beautiful auburn hair.

"So much for your Queen Bee tactic," I yelled at Jean over the noise of the scene.

"I don't know," Jean said. "Look."

He pointed at Keiko, who had pulled out her sword, raising it above her head like the valkyrie warrior she was—like the leader she was. Keiko was issuing orders and gathering the troops into some semblance of order. Her words cut through the chaos, and the surprised Others went from shocked and easy prey to a coherent, collected fighting unit, cutting off the advantage of the advancing army much earlier than expected.

The storm giant at the marquee leapt into the air and grabbed onto the ankle of a red dragon. Blue energy and red fire coursed out of them as they unleashed their fury. Giant vs. dragon, lightning vs. fire … I got my fight, and it was horrific. All I could see were two magnificent creatures of ancient lore and legend killing each other for the belief that their purpose mattered more than the other's.

Lazlo whistled for Pegasus, who flew in from only the GoneGods knew where and the leshy jumped onto the winged legend's back. "Go. We'll do our best to shield you until you are out of the camp," he said, taking to the sky where three aswangs met him.

The leshy swung his wooden club, knocking two out of the sky before the third one bit down on his neck. Reaching behind him with his free arm, he peeled the creature off him. The aswang took chunks of grass-green flesh and blood with her as she plummeted to the earth. "Go!" he screamed, touching his wound. "Go while you can."

"Damn it," I yelled as Jean threw me a shotgun.

Then, darting into the thick brush of the forest, the two of us ran away from the danger of the camp and toward the greater threat of rising gods and their fanatical servants.

I believe this is exactly what they mean by "out of the frying pan and into the fire," I thought.

It must have been one of my out loud thoughts, because Jean chuckled. "Hellelujah."

End of Part 3

PART IV
INTERMISSION

18

CHARON

WITNESSETH THE FERRYMAN

Charon has carried many from the battlefield to the next life, but he has never been in a battle himself.

Nor has death ever been a threat. But now he finds himself in the midst of a battle unlike any he has ever seen. Others fighting Others— not for their gods, but for something far less defined. To claim a future for this world that neither side can clearly see.

Invocations of offensive magic fill the air with a low but pervasive thrum of death. Others fall. A giant leaps up to bring down a red dragon. The two had embraced in deadly battle, only for both to succumb to the finality of life.

Death is all around him, all the more evident in the streams of red and blue and green and yellow blood.

He watches in horror as a jinni bleeding smokeless fire pierces the heart of an angel who bleeds light; a dusty puff of brown blood seeps from a dying dwarf; a dead ice dragon drips crystalline stalagmites.

Charon feels their lives leaving them, their essences escaping the mortal coil only to go nowhere. Once upon a time, he would have chaperoned them all to the next place. But in a world where there is no next place, all he can do is watch helplessly as more and more life fades into nothing.

The sensation is overwhelming and Charon falls to his knees, scurrying away on hand and foot. You would think that a reaper such as he would not be frightened by death, but all Charon feels is fear.

Fear, not only for his own death—certainly that is there—but fear for the GoneGod World. For even if the fighting were to stop, how does the world heal from something as terrible as this?

Charon cowers behind a large sycamore tree. He waits. For what? He is not sure. Perhaps he is waiting for the fighting to stop. Perhaps he is waiting for an Other or a human to find him and end his suffering. Perhaps he is waiting for something else entirely.

Then he feels it: that one lost soul that refuses to fade away, but rather cries to be guided back into the body it once possessed.

A living soul that seeks its living host.

And when he sees the young girl from the hotel run into the forest beyond the camp, he knows what he is waiting for.

He knows why he is here.

Not to escort the many fallen to the Land of the Dead, but rather to guide one soul back to life.

19

WATCH HOW THEY RUN

*A*s we broke through the line of trees, I expected to see a net of Others trying to block our way. What I didn't expect was every last one of them who'd been positioned to stop our advance being taken down by the arrows and spears from our side. Turning, I saw Keiko pointing her sword in our direction. It looked like we were going to make use of Jean's Queen Bee strategy after all.

Two pterolykos, with their white wings and wolf-like bodies, followed us into the forest and I stopped running for a long second to see where Keiko was. She was still on the field, her back facing the forest. She wasn't going to join us in our quest, but rather stay behind and face the assault of the approaching army, guiding her own troops against the onslaught.

Like I said: one hell of a leader.

"You coming?" Jean said, unloading a round into the tree above him. A second later, the red body of a yara-mah-yha-who dropped to the ground.

I growled as I ran after Jean, leaping over the unconscious red Australian vampire and moving deeper into the forest. The pterolykos were right behind us, providing cover while some of the more "floral" Others stalked us. I'm talking hill trolls, dark elves and pixies.

Granted, pixies didn't seem that dangerous, but they were pack hunters who had centuries of experience using their smallness to their advantage. Think Gulliver and you'll get a sense of their tactics.

Still, Jean and I were running so fast with the pterolykos behind us that none of them really slowed us down. We were making great time, and at this pace we'd be at the hotel in a matter of minutes.

But we weren't going to the hotel, were we? We were heading toward Jean's secret passageway west of the hotel. But every time we adjusted course to head there, inevitably something would happen to force us toward the hotel.

We weren't lucky or good—the Others on Team Three Dead Gods were herding us toward a trap. Jean must have come to the same realization as me, because he abruptly stopped running.

"We're fuc—" An arrow flew so close to his shoulder that it took lint as it sailed by. Jean didn't even flinch. Rather, he threw out his arms and screamed, "Shoot me! Come on—an arrow right here should do it." He put a hard finger on his forehead. "Or here." One over his heart. "Come on."

The larger of the two pterolykos drew close to Jean. "What are you doing?" he growled, scanning the forest for more marauders.

Jean ignored it, focusing on a point in the treeline.

I didn't. "They're herding us. They won't kill us. Well, they won't kill me and him. You guys I'm not so sure."

"Humph," the pterolykos spat.

"Go back—help the others."

"But the noro priestess—"

"—told you to help, and you've done that. You've done all that you can. They will kill you. They won't kill us." I focused on where Jean was looking. "At least, not right away. Isn't that right?" I screamed. "Come out, come out wherever you are."

Three baba yagas appeared at the point we had been fixed on. Their camouflage had been so good that it looked like they had simply manifested out of nowhere.

The pterolykos lifted his bow, but I put a hand out. "No. There's no hope for you here. The only reason you're not dead is because they don't want to aggravate us. But that courtesy only works up to a point. Go. There is nothing you can do for us now. Please, just go."

The pterolykos hesitated before lifting his arm straight up and letting out a mighty roar. He turned away to rejoin the fight on the beach.

↔

Jean and I walked to the lead baba yaga, who guided us to the hotel with respect and honor. Now that our intentions to follow were clear, they saw no need to harm us. They wanted us to follow them to the hotel to … what? Have a pow-wow? Discuss the meaning of life now that three gods were coming back?

One thing was blatantly clear: for guys who wanted to help the gods rise, they didn't get the memo that I was a threat. Kind of made sense, though. The gods communicated to the Heralds through dreams and delirium. Not the most reliable line of communication, and if the message got muddled—as it often did when gods spoke to mortals—then as far as they were concerned, I was just the girl with the map.

I was also the girl who had a legitimate claim to enter the museum. For all they knew, I wanted the gods to return.

But the danger was far from over, because whatever or whoever they thought we were, these guys were smart enough to ask questions first, kill later.

And "kill later" was almost certainly on their to-do list.

20

THE BOYS IN BLACK

*T*hey took us to the camp where the zen rock garden had become a hell of a lot less zen and a hell of a lot more prisoner-campy. A large, makeshift pen housed all the Others who had either fought against those who worshipped the Three Who Are One, or who had simply come to the Celestial Solace Hotel for a holiday. Either way, no one was in five-star accommodations anymore.

From the ground, the view of the place was a lot more real than it had been from the satellite pictures. And seeing Harry and Aki—bloodied, bruised, but intact—filled me with both relief and sadness. Neither of those Others deserved what was happening to them and by the GoneGods, I would do everything in my power to make this right.

My two battered friends gave me slight nods as their hopes I'd rescue them were dashed by me being brought through all tied up.

The baba yaga presented us to a friggin' angel who sat next to two Heralds, both of whom were humans in their characteristic robes with that thousand-yard stare in their dazed eyes. I recognized them from the alleyway and our fight with the nio back on Okinawa.

From the way the three of them sat, a position of prominence hadn't been given to any one of them. Rather, they sat around more like an elder council. And given two of them were insane, this trip was turning out to be a bit more progressive than practical.

"Welcome, welcome," the angel said, light literally beaming out of him. He looked like a glow-in-the-dark figurine, his white skin and wings reflecting the little light the moon offered. Up close, I saw that he was an ordinary angel—not an archangel, seraph or cherub. Up in Heaven, this guy would have been a worker bee whose primary purpose was worshipping the Big Guy in all the forms He took.

Jean took a seat in front of the council. "The name's Jean. Jean-Luc Matthias—and before you say it, I know all about the missing Mark, so let's skip it. And you are?" He gestured at the angel.

"My name does not concern you," the angel said. "But for simplicity's sake, you may call me Daniel. After all, he was the first of your kind to mention one of my kind by name. And given how much He was into letting you talking monkeys do all the naming, it's only fitting."

"Humph," I said, sitting next to Jean. "Angels and their names. You know he won't tell us his real name because he thinks that'll give us power over him. It might have once, but with the gods gone—"

"God," Daniel corrected.

"*Gods* gone"—I hissed the *s* to emphasize the plurality of their departure—"I don't think the whole name-and-power thing still works. You're holding on to a dead past."

"Perhaps," Daniel said. If my words bothered him, he made no show of it. "But I find in this faithless new world, its best to hold on to something, don't you think? Nonetheless, these two fine fellows are Hosea and Gomer, named after the prophets of old."

"Wonderful to meet you," Jean said. "Now, if we can cut to it, I'd like to start with the burning question of the day. Why didn't you kill us?"

Daniel lifted a curious eyebrow. "Why did you assume I ever wanted to kill you?"

"Well, we're kind of on opposite sides here," Jean said.

Jean's question was fair. Because of their attack, we didn't have time to prepare, instead darting out on a suicide run through the forest, where the only chance of success would have been because they messed up.

They hadn't, which meant that they'd had plenty of chances to kill us. But they also didn't do that, either. My only guess was that they had no idea about my soul and the power I held in the Shinto Land of the Dead.

But just because you don't think an enemy is a threat doesn't mean you don't take them out. Any experienced tactician knows that the fewer grunts there are around to muck up your plans, the better. The only reason we were alive was because they wanted something from us. But what? I couldn't imagine.

The angel processed Jean's words and I could see him deciding what he should say in response. But as I threw my gaze at Daniel, looking for any clue as to the mystery of our continued breath, I got nothing.

Way to go, Detective Darling.

It wasn't just my lack of detective skills that were playing against us. It was also the fact that we were dealing with a friggin' angel. And reading angels was hard to do; their subconscious tics were so customized to who they once were in Heaven or Hell that there were no common, tell-tale signs amongst them. Each was as unique as a snowflake and each carried themselves with the personalized mission of their past. To understand what made Daniel tick, I needed to know who he once was.

Trouble was, he knew that, too. Hence the false name.

"We may be on opposite sides of the war, but are we on opposite sides of the *mission*? I think not," the angel said.

"Are we talking military mission, personal mission, company mission? Missionaries? You're not going to hand me a pamphlet, are you?" Jean sneered. "But missions aside, what's your deal, anyway? Aren't you an angel of God? So what are you doing worshipping three dead gods from debunked religions? Shouldn't you be evangelizing or something? Or are you one of those guys who's promiscuous with his faith? You know, willing to give it up for the first god that shows up and—"

If you ever want to get into a fight with an angel, just question their faith, and that was exactly what Jean's rant was meant to do. He'd wanted to goad Daniel into losing his temper or worse, trying to get the angel to slip up and do something stupid. It was a classic move, the old escape-the-basement-by-pissing-off-the-psychopath tactic, and I would have applauded Jean's efforts if we were actually locked in a basement.

We weren't. We were in the middle of an enemy camp, surrounded by combatants.

But Daniel didn't get angry. He didn't even express any emotion. He just stared at Jean as he ranted. He was so devoid of emotion that I double-checked his wings just to make sure we were actually speaking to an angel and not some other kind of winged Other.

Feathery white wings ... definitely an angel, I thought.

Since I couldn't read Daniel, I turned to Hosea and Gomer to see if there was anything there. Gomer stared impassively straight ahead. He wasn't looking at either of us, just sitting as still as a human was capable of, his hands folded in his lap. Hosea, on the other hand, swayed back and forth, muttering something to himself that I couldn't make out.

"We all serve God in our own way," Daniel said as soon as Jean finished his rant.

"And how is he serving God?" I asked, gesturing at Hosea. "What's his role in all this?"

"Hosea is receiving another vision from the Three Who Are One," Daniel said, as if Hosea were receiving a phone call. "He will be with us soon enough, as soon as he establishes a connection."

"To what? The hotel's Wi-Fi?" Jean's voice dripped with venom. "I can give you the password, if you like."

"No, that will not be necessary," Daniel said. Rising, he gestured to two centaurs standing nearby. "Come, make our guests less comfortable and bring them to my tent. I need to examine them more closely to see if they are worth keeping around." Daniel stepped away, but then paused, cocking his head in Hosea's direction. "Also, if he finally has anything new to say, be sure to call me immediately."

. . .

↔

We were led to a marquee tent of the other Other camp. Based on its gold rim and floral design, it was probably used by the hotel for weddings—not war councils—and given its central location, I guessed this was where Daniel liked to hold council and do other minion*ie* things.

The centaurs dropped us into the middle of the room, where Daniel stood with his back to us. "Leave us," he said, and the centaurs snorted before stomping away.

Alone, Jean looked up at the angel. "You know, we're not really into this. I mean, you're cute, but we're both in committed relation-ships and you're kind of a dick, so …"

"Always with the jokes," he said, his voice droning as he spoke. "Jokes used as shields to hide from your fear. But one such as you, Jean-Luc Matthias, should not hide from your fear. You should embrace it."

The angel turned, and his eyes went solid black. I'm not talking like someone tattooed his eyeballs with black ink. This was more of a let's-replace-my-eyeballs-with-the-empty-void-of-night   kind   of black.

Daniel's eyes widened as he swayed his head between us, staring at Jean and me. It wasn't so much the way he was looking at us, but the way he *wasn't* looking at us that bothered me. It was as if he was looking through us to see what was behind us.

No, that wasn't right either. It was as if he was using us as a filter to see what he needed to see. Like 3D-movie glasses, we were what brought whatever he was searching for into focus.

But that wasn't the strangest bit. The truly weird thing was that he was clearly not using magic to do whatever he was doing, but he showed some signs of burning time.

Jean must have noticed that, too, because he looked at his Mickey Mouse watch and counted in his head before whispering, "My watch isn't speeding up."

So this angel wasn't burning time, which mean he was doing his "thing."

Some Others have a "thing." An ability that is innate and part of their being. Things can vary, but generally go by time. Take the ly erg as an example. I met one of those fae soldiers a few weeks back and learned that ly ergs can use their dying breath to grant them a single wish (as long as the dying breath was taken on the battlefield).

Not all Others have a thing, but if they do, it tends to be along species' lines. But angels are different; each angel had their own thing. And that thing was directly associated with whatever purpose they were created to fulfill.

And Daniel was doing his thing. Trouble was, I didn't know what his thing was.

After a few minutes of him staring at us with two black pits, he smirked before his eyes returned to normal. "Good," he said with a smile.

Jean, who was rattled like I was, said, "What the hell was that? Did you just black-hole-sun us?"

"I don't think that's a thing," I said. "But whatever he did do is his *thing*, isn't it? And given that things are related to purpose, and your purpose for being is clearly to be an asshole, I'm guessing you just created a list of cutting insults to bore us with."

"Actually," Daniel began, leaning in close. The void was gone, and normal eyes stared down at me. "I just wanted to make sure you two were a part of it."

"A part of what?" Jean asked.

"Why, the end, of course. I saw The End of Everything and both of you were there."

21

SEEKING A FRIEND FOR THE END
OF THE WORLD

"*W*hen God made me, He imbued my very essence with the ability to see the end, then He asked me to find all who would be there and make sure that those who are a part of the end will be present for the final moments in time. I can look into the hearts and souls of humans and know who will be there at the last moment of all. And I see both of you there," Daniel said, clapping his hands together. "Oh, happy days. Happy, happy days."

"So that's why you're here? To help usher in the apocalypse? What about worshipping the Three Who Are One?"

"Bah, humbug. Those faithless fools outside run around hoping, praying that the return of Baldr, Quetzalcoatl and Izanami will also mean the return of their immortality." He spat out the dead gods' names like he was spitting out sand. "They do not understand what Three Who Are One's true purpose is. They return to fulfill God's final wish: to end it all." Daniel's eyes lit up as he rose to his feet and began pacing the marquee with rapid, excited steps.

"But I wasn't sure if they would actually *be* the end. After all, so much has changed since the gods left and I wasn't entirely sure the old prophesies would come true. After all, it is by God's decree that human hands will be instrumental to ending it all. But no humans were on the island, and I grew fearful that I would have to suffer this world even longer." He wiped away imagined dirt from his left shoulder.

"But when I heard two humans were on the island, my heart swelled with hope." More light-filled tears swelled in eyes that, only moments ago, had been impossibly dark. "That is why I commanded that you two be unharmed and brought to me. I needed to see you both for myself, see if I could find confirmation in your presence and … and I have. You both shall be part of the end." He clapped his hands together, raising them to the sky, his once-caught tears painting streams of light down his cheeks. "The end is near. Finally, God's command will be fulfilled."

Something didn't make sense, and as much as I knew not to question the crazed, homicidal killer during the middle of a crying fit, I couldn't help myself. "Aren't the Heralds human?" I asked. "I mean, couldn't you do your whole black, dead-eyed trick on them to see if this was the end?"

Daniel cocked his head to one side as if truly confused by my question. That, or he simply couldn't believe I was so ignorant. "They are prophets," he said, like that explained everything.

"So?" I gestured for him to go on.

"Prophets are more human than human. That is the gift of being touched by divinity. It makes them …"—he paused as he searched for the word—"immune to one such as me."

So that's why he didn't kill us. He thinks we're a part of the apocalypse. Or that the apocalypse needs a couple humans around at the end. Potatoes, po-tah-toes, I suppose. Either way, he believes that humans need to be present at the end.

I thought about the army of Others battling on the beaches of this Okinawan island. They were fighting for a new beginning. Granted, that new beginning included three egotistical, evil gods, but given all they'd endured these last four years, could you blame them? If these gods turned out to be a mistake, then they were simply trading one shitty life for another. I was pretty sure that was the definition of "nothing to lose."

But they were fighting for life. Fighting for a better tomorrow. None of them knew that this asshole of an angel was using them to fight for no tomorrow at all. It was never about finding new gods or regaining his immortality.

It was about fulfilling what Daniel believed to be God's final wish: to end everything.

To end everything, I mused. *It must be strange to want to destroy everything you've built, even for a god. But if that's what you wanted, you'd think you'd want to do it yourself, right? Build it with your hands, end it with your hands— that kind of thing. I just don't get it. If God really wanted this to all go away, and He's all powerful, then why not end it all when He left?* I thought, and from the way both Jean and Daniel turned to look at me, it had been out loud.

"He, in His divine wisdom, ordained that you humans have a chance to get your eternal souls in order before the end. His mercy has given you all one last chance at salvation. One last chance to prove yourself worthy before the end of all."

"And how exactly did He do that?"

"Those who faithfully, unwaveringly worshipped Him after His departure will be rewarded with life eternal," Daniel said.

"Like you?" Jean cut in.

"Like me," Daniel said, his face glowing with the fervor of one who truly believed he was saved.

↔

"So"—Jean turned to me—"seems like we're a part of the end."

"Well, my mother always said I would be the death of her. I guess what she meant to say was that I'd be the death of *everyone*, including her."

Jean chuckled before shaking his head. "I don't know. I mean, this guy talks a big game, but somehow I just don't know. If God wanted to end everything, He would have ended everything. Why get three second-rate gods to do His dirty work for Him? Why go through all this drama of leaving, but not really leaving, just to see who will remain faithful? A lot of wishful thinking ..."

I nodded in agreement. "If wishes were horses and all that jazz," I said, looking Daniel straight in the eye. "And have you considered that your first concern might have been the right one? You weren't sure if old prophesies still held. Maybe 'old angel things' don't hold, either. Two wrongs don't make a right; two wrongs just make you more wrong."

I didn't know if this was us goading him into making a mistake, or just letting off some steam, but either way, if felt good to kick this guy in the ribs ... metaphorically speaking.

"And what's more, I spoke to those three gods," I said. "When I was in the museum, I spoke to them. And other than being total jerks, do you know what they have in common? None of them believe that they're ending anything. They all believe that once they resurrect themselves, they will rule over this world unchallenged. Forever. I've been hearing a lot of apocalypse chatter—and not just from you, Daniel—and I find it all hard to believe. Vague prophesies aside, what do you know that they don't? Dead or not, they are, after all, gods. And you're just an angel."

Daniel was rattled, his joy replaced by a slow, simmering anger. "God made me in the beginning and the first words He spoke to me were to tell me that I would be present at the end. That I, of all the angels, would be instrumental in ushering in His will. Then He kissed my forehead and I felt a divine love unlike—"

"—anything you've felt before or since," I said. "Or maybe you were going for, 'unlike anything you humans are capable of feeling.' We get it. But herein lies the rub, dear Daniel: He left. That was the 'end' He was talking about ... His departure. And guess what? You were here to witness it. You are here witnessing it right now."

I tried to get to my feet as I drilled my words into the angel, soaking them with as much anger as I felt in my still soul-less body. I knew I was pushing him to the edge, going beyond the point of angering him so he'd make a mistake and we could escape.

I was pushing him to kill me. And I didn't care.

"But the end isn't some dramatic event with trumpeting horns and broken seals," I spat. "No, this end is the slow-burning, perpetual dying that comes with mortality. That's how He's ending it. Ended it. He kept His promise to you when He left you behind. Tell me, did He say anything about you surviving the end? I don't think so. If He did, you would still be in Heaven—"

"Enough!" Daniel screamed, pulling out his sword and grabbing me by my neck. He placed his blade against my throat; he only needed to apply a bit of pressure and slice to one side and I'd be done. Then, so much for me being a part of the end. Would my death be enough to ruin the apocalypse? Probably not, but if there was a one-percent chance of stopping it if I stopped breathing, then I had to take it.

But Daniel didn't slit my throat. Instead he rubbed a grubby, sweat-filled hand over my face before dropping me to the ground. "Enough," he whispered. "Enough. This is the end. I have faith that it is, and I will not allow one such as you to fill my heart with doubt. I cannot—"

There was a bray at the tent's entrance. "Hosea, he is speaking."

"Oh good," Daniel said, not breaking his furious eye contact with me. "Let's go see what our gods have to say, shall we?"

2 2

THEY DON'T MAKE PROPHETS
LIKE THEY USED TO

We were dragged out of the tent and put in front of Hosea, who swayed back and forth just like he had when I'd first seen him in the izakaya. He was murmuring something in a low tone as Gomer sat next to him, eyes closed, not saying or doing anything. Made me wonder why they kept Gomer around, if all he did was … nothing.

Hosea's low hum turned into a high-pitched squeal as his face contorted in pain. He dug his fingers into his forehead, clawing at his own skin like he was trying to dig into his brain. Thin streams of blood ran down, and as if that wasn't gross enough, he clawed downward, digging eight crimson-colored streams down his face.

Then he stopped moving as if he hadn't just given himself a Freddy Krueger makeover.

Gomer began to speak. "The time draws near," he said, his voice distorted and inhuman. "Soon our powers will be great enough to break free of this place and—"

"Yeah, yeah," I said. "Really, Daniel—this is what you brought us out to hear? 'Time draws near …' 'Soon, our powers …' These lines are out of a b-movie, at best. You'd think after millions of years, you'd learn to avoid the clichés and come up with something original—"

My mini-rant was abruptly cut off by Gomer, who opened his eyes and looked at me. Recognition came over his face, but not because he was remembering me from earlier … it was like he actually *knew* me. Like we were two long-lost friends accidently meeting up in the middle of Times Square.

But any friendliness was short-lived, as Gomer's face filled with hatred and he cried out, "You brought her here? Fools. Kill her. Now. Now. Now." Gomer repeated the word over and over again, and from the way he cried out, I knew he wasn't going to stop until either he was dead, or I was. So it seemed that Gomer did do stuff … like ordering my execution. And given I was hogtied and on my knees, I was guessing me dead was more likely.

One of the centaurs who had tied us up charged forward without hesitation and unsheathed his sword. They were getting ready to run me down and given the position I was in, there was literally nothing I could do.

"No!" cried Daniel. I guessed the apocalypse hadn't started in earnest and he needed me around a wee bit longer to help usher in the end.

But any power Daniel had was nothing compared to the authority their nutbar of a prophet had, and neither centaur slowed down.

"Oh hell no," Jean said, before clamping down hard with his teeth. Then he lunged forward, knocking me down just in time for the centaur's blade to fly over us.

Jean had saved me, but for what? So I could live another minute or so? I waited as I heard the centaur turning for another pass at me, while Gomer's cries continued to fill the air, accented by the clicking of hooves that sounded more like the ticking of a clock counting down the last seconds of my life.

The centaur stood above us, getting ready to drive his sword through both our bodies.

"No," Daniel said. "Just the girl." He spoke like just killing me was the lesser of two evils.

How chivalrous, I thought as the centaur reached down and pulled Jean off me.

"Bastards. God damned bastard," Jean spat, and given that there was no quip, no ill-timed joke, I knew I was a goner.

To Jean's credit, he struggled against the beast, but in the end, the half-horse, half-man threw him off me with all the exertion necessary to fling a sack of potatoes. Jean went tumbling away.

So this is how it ends for me, I thought, and readied myself for the nothing that would come after.

↔

When I was a young girl, my mother—who was a God fearing, church-going Christian back then—told me that I had a guardian angel watching over me. I believed that until the day I was turned into a vampire. After that, I chalked up concepts like "guardian angels" and "divine intervention" to superstitions held by people too weak to save themselves. In other words, my mother was wrong.

Dead wrong.

But it seemed I was the one who was wrong, because just before the centaur could drive his blade through me, dozens of mokumokuren appeared. And not just mokumokuren ... the futakuchi-onna from the plane, the three specter salarymen from the izakaya and dozens of other half-dead, ghostly Others.

Gabriel—my guardian angel—and his half-dead army had shown up to save me.

And save me they did. From the centaur at least, because although the ghosts weren't corporeal in any meaningful punch-you-in-the-face-with-a-solid-fist kind of way, they served up one hell of distraction.

The horse part of the centaur took hold; the mythical beast reared up on his hind legs as he tried to swat away the floating eyeballs.

Daniel lunged toward me, but before he could get within striking range, Gabriel manifested. Except it wasn't him, it was a projection, a hologram (not that magic needs a scientific explanation). The real Gabriel was still nailed to a cross and from the grimaced expression on this hologram, he was still in a hell of a lot of pain.

Seeing the archangel, Daniel dropped to his knees. "Gabriel," he said. "You're dead. I *saw* you die. I—"

Gabriel lifted a silencing hand and spoke six words to Daniel. Six words that stopped the angel dead in his tracks. "Father would not have wanted this."

Hearing those words from Gabriel must have been like being hit by a truck, because Daniel half-crumpled and shook his head as streams of light fell from his eyes. "I was only doing His will … I was only doing His will."

Devastated, babbling angels aside, there were other dangers to contend with. Specifically, prophets.

If Hosea and Gomer had noticed the ghostly Others, they made no show of it. Their eyes were intently focused on me as they crossed their arms against their chests.

I heard a familiar rumbling. They were summoning their nio and shisa warriors, but at least this time I understood what was happening, and seeing my chance, I got up on my bound feet and did the only thing I could think of doing: I hopped over to Gomer and head-butted him hard enough to knock him out.

Hosea was backing away from me, his murmuring continuing as the thunderous rampage of the stone guardians grew louder. I saw the first of the approaching army crash through the hotel's front door as I hobbled toward the summoning prophet. But Hosea kept backing away and I knew that I wasn't going to make it in time to stop him.

I'd need a miracle to take him down. Miracles were in short supply these days, but they weren't gone—not entirely—and my miracle took the form of what looked like a giant, hairy beanbag that dropped from the sky, smothering Hosea under its incredible weight.

Aki stood triumphant over his, ahem … sack. Beneath it lay a possibly dead, definitely unconscious Hosea who was no longer summoning his guardians.

The shisa and nio, who had been approaching in force, abruptly stopped, turning back into what they normally were: lifeless statues that felt oddly appropriate in Aki's stone garden.

Jean waved over to me as he stood, gasping for breath next to the cage that once held Aki, Harry and the Others.

Harry, now free, used his immense strength to snap my binds, and the four of us stood together as we surveyed the scene.

Daniel and the centaur guards, outnumbered and no longer with their leader, were being rounded up by their once-upon-a-time prisoners. The ghostly Others and Gabriel, seeing that the situation was now under control, had gone, presumably to preserve their limited strength in the corporeal world.

"So," I said, "that was close."

Jean stared at me gravely, like he couldn't believe I still breathed. Then he smiled and with a "I don't know—I figured I still had a few seconds to spare" and a chuckle, I knew things were right.

Well, not right. There were still the resurrecting gods to contend with. But things were better, at the very least.

"Now what?" Harry asked as he wiped dirt from his glasses.

Jean and I filled the yeti and tanuki in as quickly as possible, telling them about the gods and bombs, before Jean finally said what I had been thinking. "The path is clear. We get you inside and you do your soul magic and ... well, we call it a day."

"And the bombs?" I asked.

"Well, there is that. But how about we deal with one problem at a time? First we kill the gods dead. Then we find a bomb shelter or something."

I looked at my watch and shook my head. "No, not yet. We still have three days until they rise. There has got to be a way we can save the Others battling on the beach. Others on *both* sides," I said, emphasizing the plurality of my intention. "We have to warn them, at least. Let them know what's happening."

"We can't save them all," Jean said. "We don't have time. Hell, I doubt we even have the time to save ourselves."

"We have to—"

Harry put a hand on my shoulder. "Your capacity to love is

immense," the yeti said. "But the soldier is right: there is no time. Go. Aki and I will try to warn them, though I do not think they will listen."

Harry took a few steps toward the hotel as he spoke, as if his steps would somehow inspire me to take my own. "The passion of battle, even a battle that is being lost, is too great to be ignored and—"

But before the kind and gentle yeti could finish his thought, a giant hand burst out of the hotel, splintering the ancient structure into tinder before slamming down and squashing Harry under its incredible weight.

The gods were here.

23

IDLE, GODLY HANDS, PLAYGROUNDS AND ALL THAT JAZZ

*I*f the giant hand knew it had crushed one of the most gentle, erudite creatures I'd ever met, it made no sign of it. I had no time to mourn Harry's death; that would have to come later. Now I needed to focus on the impossibility of what was happening. How was it they had risen so quickly? We were supposed to have days left to stop them. But here one had risen out of the hole.

The hand pulled back, dragging ravines ten feet deep as fingertips wider than great sequoias clawed at the earth. From the motion, I knew it was climbing. As in, the gods, or at least one of them, was pulling himself out of the giant hole caused by the incomplete temporal transfer that occurred when our two planes of existence had overlapped.

Jean and I stood in awe as the hand of god continued clawing at the edge of the abyss while it slowly rose from beneath. A god was raising, and it took everything in my three hundred years of experience not to fall to my knees and grovel in awe-struck insanity. I totally got why everyone in an H.P. Lovecraft novel goes crazy. Seeing a god—as in, actually *seeing* one—is mind-bogglingly overwhelming.

Aki, the divine judge and tanuki of old, had seen one before and wasn't quite as flabbergasted as we were. He traded out a gaping mouth and disbelief with a well-timed, "Ah, crap. They're early. Unfashionably so."

Gallows humor. It had saved me more than once and at that moment, Aki's casualness was enough to jolt Jean and me awake. With a chuckle, we both shook our heads, looked at each other with a let's-get-to-it resolve and sprang into action.

Not that we had many actions to take. I mean, what were you supposed to do against something as huge as that? We were literally the size of fruit flies compared to what was coming out of the hole. The only thing that gave me a modicum of hope was the way the hand struggled. Whoever controlled this body wasn't used to it.

It wavered too much, moved with the uncertainty of one learning to skate without ever having seen someone skate before. If this god was struggling that much to get out, then maybe, just maybe we could get back inside where my soul-power would have a chance against it.

Then again, maybe not.

"Still, early or not, this shouldn't be. They shouldn't be at full power yet. This shouldn't be possible," the tanuki said.

"Probably not," Jean said. "But then again, there is only one of them. Maybe the other two, I don't know, gave her some of their mojo so she could rise early and deal with any threats, as in ..." He pointed at me.

"And she has the Soul Jar around her neck. She was the one who found it, used it to free them," I said. "Maybe that has something to do with it."

"Whatever the reason, what do we do now?" Jean asked.

I looked up at the massive hand struggling to find a grip and then at our surroundings. There had to be something that we could use against this god to slow it down. Then I saw my answer standing off in the distance. "Water," I said, pointing to the water tower near the hotel. "Let's make this as slippery as possible."

"On it," Aki said, twirling his massive satchel around and taking to the air. With a single bound that would have made Superman jealous, he plowed through one of the tower's legs and sent the thing toppling over, releasing gallons upon gallons of water.

"Jean, you release the prisoners—"

"They'll turn on us."

"They'll die if they can't run. This god is flailing about. It's only a matter of time until she swats them."

Jean nodded in understanding. Best to give them a chance than let them die like caged animals. "OK, and after that? What do we do?"

"We fight," I said.

"A bit more specific?"

"Well personally," I said, "I kind of want to slay some gods."

↔

Looking over at the hole, I saw our make-it-muddy gambit had paid off. The hand disappeared into the abyss below.

I was about to run over to the hole when Jean stopped me, fumbling in his pocket he pulled out Father Time's note. "I figure this is as good a time as any," he said as he unfolded it. My heart raced with anticipation and hope that the words on that paper would change everything. But when Jean's face furled with disappointment and exasperated rage, I knew hope wasn't here.

"What does it say?" I asked, expecting something cryptic and useless.

" 'Not all time is equal.' " Jean crumpled up the paper and tossed it aside.

"Fan-friggin-tastic," I muttered. "I hate it when I'm right."

But useful message from crazy Father Time or not, I didn't have time to worry about it now. Right now, I had to stop a god.

I gave Jean a hug in the way one does when things are truly over, and ran to the edge of the hole before he could say anything else. Peering down, I saw that the hand had retreated from the flow of water, presumably to find some kind of grip or footing to climb out.

I wasn't sure what I was going to do to stop it, and figured my only chance was to get down into the museum and use my soul-power to try and pull it back inside. My plan, if you could call the extreme parkour insanity I was about to attempt a "plan," was to climb down the huge god and get inside as quickly as possible.

But from where I stood, I couldn't see anything. The arms of the god, her head ... nothing. Just a dark hole that was impossibly deep.

I need to get down—quick. Jumping down would be suicide, I thought, but not seeing a god on which to climb down had basically ruined my plan. I needed access to the museum now. But without a clear path, it would take me hours to get there. *Then again, this was always a suicide mission ...*

I took ten steps back and ran to the edge, jumping into the black abyss below.

↔

Sometimes you just have to take the leap, and doing so pays off. And that was exactly what happened at that moment, for as I fell into the darkness, a body shot up through the hole. A huge, imposing body with a necklace holding a jar on it. Izanami.

So she was the one who'd come early to the party.

24

SEASONS OF THE ABYSS

Climbing down a giant goddess is harder work than you'd think. For one thing, they don't have clothes. Sure, Izanami was robed in something that covered her fun bits and displayed the majesty that was her ... but it wasn't like the robes were made of cotton.

The material (I had no idea what it was made out of) seemed to be an extension of her, something that grew out of her being. And given that Izanami was the zombie of a dead goddess, a god that was locked away by her husband Izanagi because she was too hideous to look at, the material I clung onto was covered in a mixture of old, coagulating bodily fluids that made me yearn for a full-body exfoliation with sandpaper.

Still, a girl has to do what a girl has to do, and I shimmied down the curtain of slime, making my way down the mess she called a wardrobe until I made it to the platform, but couldn't go any further to the door. It seemed that once we were actually in the waiting area in front of the museum, her clothes and body became less tangible and more ghost-like, the rest of her body trailing into the museum like a genie's tail coming out of a lamp.

The door no longer hung there, but rather had been splintered by what I can only assume was Izanami's dramatic exit.

I tried to use Izanami's ghostly tail to climb to the entrance, but my hands went right through her, and I stared helplessly from the wrong side of the chasm. I needed to get inside, but the gulf between where I stood and the entrance was too far to jump and the bridge that had once stood between the two points had been cut down by Benkei to stop me from entering.

Speaking of Benkei. I turned to see the samurai ("Warrior monk!" I heard Keiko cry in my head) standing several feet behind me, his blades around him, each dripping with a different color of blood. And not just his weapons ... his clothes were covered in so much brightly colored blood that his monk's robes looked as though they'd been tie-dyed.

And that's when it hit me: there had been Others down here trying to get in and according to Jean and Keiko, Benkei hadn't tried to stop them. But whatever stalemate they had had gone out the window when Izanami made her move, freeing the warrior monk to do what he did best. Kill.

And kill he must have done, because there wasn't a single body anywhere to be seen. I only needed to follow the rainbow-colored streams to know where the bodies were, too. They'd been dumped down the chasm.

Holy guacamole—he literally took down dozens of Others and he didn't have a scratch on him. And here I was, little old me, with no weapons, because in my haste, I figured I only needed my soul-power to stop the gods. I'd forgotten all about him.

I stared up at the giant man, waiting for him to make his move, but he didn't do anything except stare directly ahead at the door. There was fire in his eyes and I followed his gaze. Then it hit me who he really was.

Lifting my hands up, I said in my best Japanese, "You know, all this time I thought you were a guardian. But you're not, are you? You're a guard. A warden, to be more specific. You're here to make sure that whatever is in there doesn't get out."

Benkei's gaze shifted to me for a split second before he returned to his vigil. That was all the confirmation I needed.

"I'm trying to stop them from getting out, but I need your help. I need to get inside."

The warrior monk didn't move and for a long moment, I thought he wasn't going to do anything one way or another. Frustrated by his impassivity, I walked over to the edge, trying to find a way inside, when I heard heavy footsteps behind me. I turned to see Benkei charging at me, and from the way he ran, he meant to knock me into the chasm. I banked to the right, seeking to tumble out of the way, but the warrior monk was too fast and grabbed me by the collar of my shirt before leaping in the air.

This once-upon-a-time human, now divine warden, leapt over a chasm that was easily twelve yards wide like he was hopping over a babbling brook. And before I had a chance to say, "What the f—?" he threw me in the museum.

I tumbled down the hall, almost slipping in the void before righting myself. Up close to the entrance, I saw Izanami's incorporeal essence slowly flowing out of the void. She wasn't fully out yet, but she would be soon.

Benkei did not enter with me. He did, however, toss me his naginata, the bladed spear sliding across the floor toward me.

"Hell yeah," I said, picking up the weapon. I bowed deeply toward the warrior monk. He returned my bow with one of his. Formalities done, I turned to face the void so that I could kick some godly ass.

↔

I jumped into the void, naginata in hand, and as I did, I searched for a light or something to show me where the gods were at. But in the endless darkness, I couldn't see anything. They were hiding.

They had to be.

141

So I did the only thing I could think of: I turned on the lights. I focused my will like I had done the first time I faced off against the gods.

But nothing happened.

I tried again, this time adding a wee bit of gravitas to my efforts.

Nothing.

"Let there be light," I cried out.

Still nothing.

Whatever powers I seemed to have before were gone now. And just when I was starting to panic over my sudden ineffectuality, I heard a thousand voices chirp, "Your soul isn't here anymore. We gave it to our sister, Izanami, so that she may rise and clear the way for our own ascensions."

"GoneGod damn it," I cursed.

25

A BRIEF INTERLUDE FROM CHARON

*R*unning away is not something that Charon is accustomed to. Normally it is others who run from him, but now that Charon is mortal, he finds himself running for his life and, as it becomes clear what is happening here, the lives of everyone else on this planet.

He is behind the girl and her escorts, and although they are too consumed with their blind mission to see the trap being laid before them, Charon is not. He sees the woodland Others as they goad them down a path and toward a trap. He watches as they walk into it and he knows that he is powerless to help.

So at the forest's edge, Charon watches as the two humans are questioned, then taken into a large tent. He does something that he *is* used to doing.

He waits.

↔

Charon doesn't have to wait long for what comes next. He watches as the Others try to kill the girl, followed by the appearance of Gabriel and the half-dead Others. He witnesses the exchange between the angel and Gabriel, and knows that the latter is shaming the former. It is the angelic way when one of them strays off the very narrow path their god has provided them.

Finally, Charon observes Izanami's resurrection, the goddess rising from below.

The human girl has jumped into the hole. Presumably she is chasing her soul, but this is a fool's errand, for her soul is no longer in the Kami Subete Hakubutsukan. It is in the Rooh Ina'ah—the Soul Jar —that hangs around Izanami's neck.

Foolish girl. She is running from the place she should be.

So Charon continues waiting, not sure what he must do next. He is not the only one; Izanami also waits. She waits for the other two gods to join her. Waits for her powers to grow in this new world.

Waits for the moment she will be strong enough to truly rise.

↔

And in her waiting, many things happen. It starts when the angel, freed by the other human, takes to the air. Charon watches as the creature who so desperately wanted to see these gods rise shoots above him and toward the beach. Why? Charon can only guess it's a form of penance.

For that is what angels were created to do: serve, or redeem.

And when, several minutes later, the two opposing armies join forces against the rising god, Charon knows that this angel sacrificed much to turn the tides of war.

Too bad it is too late.

A lechy riding the legendary Pegasus charges at Izanami, the angel by his side, while the armies below lob every ounce of weaponry and magic at the god. It is all in vain, for as weak as she may be, she is still a goddess.

And goddesses are an immutable force that cannot be killed by blade, volley or magic.

She swats the ground. The tremors break the earth apart and swallow half the army whole. Then she swats angel and lechy alike out of the air.

The angel and lechy do not survive the fall, but the legendary Pegasus does, regaining control before her body slams into the earth below.

Landing, the winged horse looks at the rising god with fury and defiance, and that is the moment when Charon finally knows his wait is over.

Now is the time for action.

↔

Picking up a fallen blade and leaping on Pegasus's back, he commands the horse to take to the air. Riding the beast is not like being on his ferry; the journey is wrought with bucks and twists, rises and falls that the ferryman would happily trade for a ride on the roughest of waters.

Charon is not built for flying.

Nor is he built for fighting.

But he understands the ways of the dead and living better than most gods, and instructing Pegasus to fly toward Izanami's neck, he gets in close enough to sever the rope that binds the Rooh Ina'ah to her.

The jar falls—not that she notices; Izanami is too busy swatting away the nuisances that are the attacking Others.

The jar falls to the ground and so does Charon, leaping after it.

Under the will of the shaking earth, the jar jumps around, flailing about until finally he manages to catch it.

Uncorking the jar, he coaxes the soul out.

But there is nowhere for the soul to go. And without his ferry, he has no means to guide it anywhere.

So the glowing essence hovers about the jar, waiting for instructions. He needs a carrier. He needs a way to get it to the girl below.

And just as Charon falters, unsure what to do next, he hears a voice ask, "Is that what I think it is?"

End of Brief Interlude

26

MORTAL KOMBAT ... THE GODS' EDITION

*S*tupid, stupid, stupid, I thought. *This is a trap. Of course it is. Take my soul outside, use the Raspy Man's soul inside. Hobble the only person who could possibly stop them. It was exactly what I would have done in their place.*

"Very good, mortal girl. One soul above, one soul below. Divide and conquer." Quetzalcoatl's thousand beaks laughed. Turning, at he and Baldr stood together, their bodies illuminated by an inner glow that I interpreted as their way of smugly relishing their victory.

Behind them floated Gabriel. The archangel was obviously in great pain, but it was more than that. He was nearly transparent, as in literally fading away. Whatever magic he had burned or powers he'd used to help us up above had cost him dearly.

The archangel tried to speak, the words coming out more like a crackling sound than anything coherent. Quetzalcoatl turned and put a shushing finger over his lips. "Shush, shush, shush. Conserve your strength," the dead god said in a caring, almost loving tone. "We don't want your essence fading into the oblivion too soon. After all, you are one of the great witnesses and it is only fitting that you are here to witness us rise."

So much for a loving tone, I thought. Pointing my spear at them, I said, "OK ... now what?"

"Now ..."—Baldr snapped his fingers, and whereas before he had been floating several yards away, he was now on me—"you die." He produced a dagger from only the GoneGods knew where and stabbed me in the stomach. "Painfully, slowly, eternally ... you die."

↔

The blade dug deep into my stomach as blood floated out of me like bubbles from a child's toy. I watched the crimson orbs drift around me and knew that I had minutes to live. Minutes—if the dead god didn't stab me again.

But from the obvious joy painted on his face, I knew that he was relishing my slow demise.

I tried to move, to fight. To use my last moments doing something useful, but I couldn't. The pain was too great, the loss of blood too fast. I was dying and the only thing I could do was go with it.

I thought of Justin and one of our pillow chats before things got weird and bad between us. He had asked me what I would do if I knew I only had five minutes to live. "How would you spend them?" he asked.

"Five minutes isn't a long enough to do or get anywhere," I'd said.

"Play," he admonished me. "Let's say you could wave a wand and be anywhere, do anything, but you only have five minutes and then nothing. What would you do with that time?"

"I don't know," I answered honestly. "I suppose I would want to see my father again."

"But he's dead."

I gave Justin a look of mock surprise. "He is?"

"Come on, be serious."

"I am. If I could do anything—you know, wave that magic wand—
I'd want to see him again. Say I'm sorry. And tell him I love him."

I coughed and I noticed that the pain in my belly was fading. That
was a bad sign. I'd been around enough death to know that the body
reaches a point of no return and usually that point comes with no
pain. The body's final gift: a peaceful passing.

I wondered how many breaths I had left. A hundred? Maybe less?
And as the darkness of the nothing that comes next washed over me, I
heard an old, familiar voice:

"Hello, Kat. It has been a long time indeed."

↔

I looked up and saw my father standing before me. He was wearing
the old family tartan and the smile he gave me every time I walked
into a room. It was my smile, his little gift to me for being me.

"Hello, my wee little Kat."

"Father," I said, my voice weak, fading. Was this the gift of death?
To see the ones you loved most before drawing your final breath?

"Aye, it is me."

"Oh Father," I said, tears welling as they threatened to burst over. "I
am so sorry. I am—"

"Katrina, enough of the self-pity," he said, his voice stern, loving.
Commanding.

"But I am sorry. Sorry for killing you. Sorry for all the pain I
caused."

"Aye, and pain you did cause. But seeing you here, seeing you now,
I see that all you have done and all that has been done to you was
perhaps for a grander purpose. You are about to kill three gods, are
you not?"

"The gods ... another item on my long list of failures. I'm done," I
said. "Done before I've done anything of worth."

149

"No, yer nae done yet, my wee Kat," he said. "Yer far from done. The road to atonement is long and hard and miserable. And, my dear daughter, yer still only at the start of it."

"I don't know that this is the start of anything. I'm dying. I'm dead. And now that the gods are gone, death is the end," I said, surprised at the relief in my voice. I was ready to die. No—that wasn't true. I was ready to rest.

"Yer nay dying," he said. "Yer only beginning."

I looked at him curiously, and placing a hand over my stomach, I drew my hand back and saw no blood. "What …?"

"Look," he said, pointing at the abyss. There I saw two unmoving gods standing statue-still. And behind them, near the entrance to the void, floated Jean, his arm frozen as if he had just thrown something. Somehow he was inside again. Whatever claim he had over this place granted him access, just like my missing soul granted me access.

My father pointed at Jean. "That man has risked much to give yer soul back."

"My soul?" I felt around me and knew that my father had spoken the truth. Seems that as soon as Jean entered this place with my soul out of the jar, I became whole again.

My soul wasn't just into the void anymore—it was in me.

"Aye, and with yer soul, they dinnae stand a chance, my wee Kat. Now, go … do what ye must."

I floated next to my father. "Is that really you? I mean, *you* you, and not just a conjuration in my mind?"

He laughed. "How can I answer that honestly? If I were a construct, I would say, 'Aye,' because that is what you would want to hear. And if I weren't, well … me answer would still be 'Aye.' "

I pursed my lips. He was right: I had no way of knowing if I had the power to actually call him to me or this was a lie that I'd created using my soul-power. Either way, I took what I could and gave him the biggest, hardest hug I could.

Some lies are best embraced.

"I love you," I said. "And I am sorry. I will make up for the wrong I have done. I will make you proud. That is my oath. My promise."

"Aye," he said, wiping away his own tears. "You are already halfway there, my wee Kat, for I am already so proud of you, my darling, my heart. My daughter." He put his hands out before him, and in them he conjured the mask of the Divine Cherubs. "Here, wear our family's clan tartan and send those fiends back to Hell."

"Aye, Father. I will."

I put on the mask and, pulling the spear before me, I searched for the spearhead of the Lance of Longinus. Having a soul in this place made the impossible possible, and I summoned the spearhead instantaneously.

Then, unfreezing time, I charged forth. Not for the world, but for the man who had twice now given me life.

↔

What happened next literally took place in less than a second. I unfroze the gods before slicing them in half with the spearhead. Damn, now I get why Michael Bay does all those slow-mo fight scenes. There was way too much cool missed.

Jean floated down. Summoning him toward me, I drew him in like a tractor beam on *Star Trek*.

"How the hell did you do that?"

"Phenomenal cosmic power! Itty bitty living space," I said, gesturing to myself.

I flew over to Gabriel and freed the archangel. But it was too late; he was so close to gone that we could hardly see him. But I had a soul in a place where souls were gods. And, knowing this, I did the soul equivalent of CPR, imbuing him with a couple pumps that brought him back to—if not life, then at least opaqueness.

The archangel, freed and whole, did not thank me, but rather floated to the door. "It is too late. She has escaped."

"Then we use this," I said, gesturing to the spear.

Gabriel shook his head. "That only kills gods who are dead or wish to die."

"All I got from that is 'No, not possible,' " I said. "So what do we do?"

"She has not fully escaped. Only part of her is outside."

Confirming the archangel's assumption, Jean said, "Only her upper body is out. The rest of her is in the hole."

"So if we can close the museum and send this plane of existence on its way," Gabriel said, "then we can—"

"No good," I said. "Aki said the rotation won't happen for a while still. Weeks, if Aki is right."

"The tanuki is rarely wrong." And with a heavy, un-angelic-like sigh, continued, "I fear all is lost."

"No. I refuse to believe that. There has to be something in the museum. Some magical item, some weapon that—" I snapped my fingers twice, pointing at Jean. "What did Father Time say again?"

"Not all time is created equal. Whatever that means."

"I think I know," I said. "And we need to get out of the void. Now."

↔

Jean didn't need to be told twice, and we left the void as fast as his karayushi-wearing ass could float. Thankfully I was there to help him along. At the entrance, I stood on the other side of the door, Izanami's ghostly essence slowly pouring through the doorway.

Gabriel joined me on the other side of the doorway. It seemed that whatever I did had brought him back from the dead. As in, literally. He was now flesh and bone. Well, flesh and feathers and talons and whatever else angels are made of.

"You're alive?"

"No," he said, "I am something in-between. Not that that matters now. Tell me, Katrina Darling, what do you plan to do?"

Standing at the open doorway, I said, "You know, you Others always say things in mysterious, cryptic ways. But that's not exactly true. What you guys really do is give us pieces of information and leave the bridging up to us." I fumbled in my pocket and pulled out the hourglass that Father Time gave me. "Bridges—like how not all time is created equal. Time flows differently in this place than outside it. Ten days in our time is … what? A minute in there?"

I flipped the hourglass so that the sand started flowing. "Father Time said this hourglass will give us all the time we need. Crazy old bat. Still, not all time is created equal, right? So let's see what happens when we force a minute of our time to happen in there." I tossed the hourglass inside and watched the thing float into the void, sand pouring through its narrow sieve.

And as the final grains fell through, the void disappeared. In its place stood a rock face with a doorway that had somehow been built inside.

A loud, thunderous boom shook the cavern we were in, like something impossibly heavy—godly heavy—had just fallen and I knew what had happened. I had forced the void to move on, and because Izanami hadn't fully exited yet, I had cut her in two.

No one survives being severed in two. No one … not even a god.

Looking at the rock face door, I also realized that I had forced the void to move on, but not the museum. That was still here, and that would have repercussions—not the least of which was the hallowed screams as the cages that once housed the worst of the worst mythical creatures rattled open.

The museum door stood wide open, its large, magical barrier hanging on the hinges. With wraithlike speed, spirits and Others that had been trapped for centuries, millennia or more—monsters that even the gods feared—poured out of the entrance and away from the museum.

I picked up Benkei's spear, ready to pursue and cut down at least a few of them, but Jean put a hand on my shoulder to stop me. "You don't stand a chance. Besides"—he pointed at his watch. Dawn was minutes away and looking through the open door I saw that Benkei was gone, presumably to pursue the worst of them—"they won't be able to get far before the bombs start dropping. Think of it as a 'when the gods open a door, we drop a bomb' kind of thing."

"That's not the expression. What do you think, Gabriel?" I asked, turning to face the angel. "Will the bombs take them down, or have we just unleashed a—"

But the angel wasn't there.

"Who are you speaking to?" Jean asked.

"Gabriel," I said, "he was right here."

"Gabriel is dead," Jean said, giving me a curious look. Then he reached out his hand. "Come on, let's get above ground. There's a dead god up there and that's not something you get to see every day."

27

IN THE ARMS OF THE ARCHANGEL

*E*ven though I had only been in the void for a couple minutes, I saw that hours had passed on the island. Whereas it had been the middle of the night before, now the early, crepuscular rays of sunlight illuminated a battlefield littered with the dead. Others of all kinds bled their sundry colors of blood.

But the gruesome sight of all the dead barely caught my attention, for in the center of the field lay Izanami, her massive body falling over the island like a mountain range. She was dead, and in death she looked beautiful. No longer was she a zombie-like creature infested with maggots the size of great danes. No longer was her skin graying and sagged. Instead, she lay like the visage of a radiant, beautiful woman, peacefully sleeping as she waited for dawn.

Dawn was approaching, and so were the human bombs.

Two very different kinds of light gonna shine down on this island, I mused.

"What?" Jean said, my out loud thoughts pulling him out of his.

"Ahh, nothing," I said, "Any chance this changes anything? You know, dead gods and all."

I turned to Jean, who stood with his tricorder in his hand. He shook his head.

"So, this is it?" I said as I headed toward the beach. "If I'm going to die, then I'm going to do it watching the sun rise. You coming?"

Jean chucked his tricorder to the ground and nodded. "I'm rarely up at dawn," he said. "Seems it would be a waste not to."

↔

We found a secluded place near the forest's edge where we would watch the rising sun. It was far enough from where the main battle had taken place that we didn't see any fallen Others. We didn't see anyone except ourselves.

The sun crept out over the horizon, lying to us that today would be a beautiful day. In the distance I could hear a soft rumble, like a rolling thunderstorm miles away. *Jets coming with their bellies full of death*, I thought, and sighed.

Today was it, but somehow I wasn't too troubled by it. After all, I'd gotten to see my father one last time. Apologize to him. And now I'd get to die like him ... staring at the rising sun.

That was what I thought about. I stole a glance in Jean's direction and saw the soldier sitting with a smile on his face.

"I'll tell you mine if you tell me yours," I said.

My words woke him from his daydream. "What?"

"That smile. I'll tell you why I'm smiling if you tell me why you are."

"Mine's simple: I'm thinking about Bella. You?"

"My dad," I said, breaking my deal by not telling him about what had happened in the void.

"You know that game you always play—how would you spend your last minutes on Earth? Turns out, you spend them doing nothing but thinking about the ones you loved most."

"Humph," I said, "there's a poet in you. Comedian? Not so much.

But a poet, yes." Then, remembering something he had said when I first met him, I said, "You know, you lost your bet."

"What bet?"

"That you'd make me laugh before this was all over. The end is nearly here and I haven't laughed yet."

Jean shrugged. "You can't win them all."

"I guess not," I said. "But you could have won this one. You didn't need to come here with Keiko and me … you could have stayed on the destroyer. Why did you join us, Jean? I mean, why did you risk your life today? You didn't have to."

Jean gave me a wry smile. "True, but if you'd failed, then it would have been the end of the world and, well … done that, been there."

I frowned, and giving him a look that simultaneously said, *"Oh, come on,"* and *"We've literally been through hell and survived. You owe me,"* I gestured for him to go on.

His cocky smile dissipated as a solemn, distant look painted his face. "I've already told you: there's this girl whom I love very much and promised to help. I keep my promises, Ms. Darling. And so do you, I suspect." He shook his head as he stared at the shoreline. "Do you think he was right? Daniel, I mean. Are we really going to be a part of the end?"

"The end didn't happen. And since we're about to bite the big one, I think not."

"Maybe. Then again," he said, "there are still a boatload of over-powered Others out there ready to take up the mantle. Maybe this was just the kick-off. A kick-off we were a part of, and in that way Daniel's 'thing' worked just fine. We *are* a part of the end—we just won't be around to see it happen."

"Pessimistic much? Remind me to not invite you to any parties," I said with a chuckle. I stared off at the rolling waves, watching the water ebb and flow on the beach as I thought about it. "You know," I eventually said, breaking the silence that hung between us, "if this is the beginning of an end still to come, then let it. I have faith that those who survive the end will just make a new beginning of it. Just like they did when the gods left. They did it once—they'll do it again. That's what I'm going to choose to believe, at least."

"Believe?"

"Yeah. That's why we're here, right? Because we both believe that this world is worth fighting for. And we're not the only ones; there are others and Others who believe the same, and their belief will carry them through."

"Ahh, belief. Well, this is another fine mess you got me into." Jean puffed on an invisible cigar as he spoke in a mock Oliver Hardy accent.

As someone who had seen Laurel and Hardy live, his impersonation was absolutely terrible. More than terrible—it was abysmally dreadful. Hilariously so.

I burst into laughter. Not just laughter, but uncontrollable guffaws that literally had me keeling over in pangs of pain. It was good to laugh, to feel again. And as I laughed, I felt my soul stir within me. It was good to be whole again, as brief as it would be.

"Hah," Jean said, leaping to his feet and doing a little victory dance. "I told you I'd have you in stitches before this ends and I did! I win. I win! I WIN!"

"I'm laughing *at* you, not with you," I said, wiping away a tear of mirth.

"Still counts, my friend. It still counts."

And indeed it did.

↔↔↔

Bombs fell, but we did not die. No living being on the island did, for before any of the humans' weapons of destruction could strike the earth, a dome shield appeared over the island and we watched as the bombs fell on the dome and fire slid down its transparent sides and harmlessly into the sea.

"How?" I asked.

"A miracle," a voice said behind me. "They are in short supply, but not gone. Not yet, at least."

"Gabriel," I said, turning to see the archangel aged to the point of death. Whatever in-between state of life and death the angel had been in, whatever magic he had left, none of that mattered, because he had used all his magic to save us. And all I could think to say as I stared at our savior was one ineffectual word: "Why?"

"The world has survived so much," Gabriel said, his ancient body becoming more incorporeal with each word. "The opening of Pandora's box, the departure of the gods. I suspect it will survive this, too. What it will not survive, however, is the loss of good men and women. Like you."

Being called "good" by an archangel—the very embodiment of good—was like being slapped in the face. Repeatedly. All I wanted to do was scream at the specter, insist that he was wrong. Wrong to save us, wrong to let out the evil.

But how do you argue with the Messenger of God? You don't. You just soak in what he has to say and have your existential crisis on your own time.

"Katrina," he said, "I have a small request for you. Here." He handed me the Soul Jar, but where it had once been the size of a witch's cauldron used to boil Hansel and Gretel, now it was barely the size of a common necklace pendant. "Take this. Go to Paradise Lot and give it to my brother, Michael. He will know what to do with it. Oh, and tell him that he is wrong—this is not the end. Just an unusual beginning."

I picked up the jar and turned to the archangel who had barely more form than the ashes of a paper lantern. Seeing that he was seconds away from oblivion, I cried out, "What about you? There must be something here that can save you."

"You, Ms. Darling, already have." And with that, Gabriel, archangel, Messenger of God and one of the Seven Mysteries, faded into nothing.

28

WHY CAN'T THIS BE THE END

he bombs didn't kill us, which meant that they didn't kill the monsters held within the museum, either. One more problem to deal with. But given how exhausted I was, it was a problem we'd deal with later.

Besides, I thought, looking over at Jean, *he's around and he's one of the good guys and he'll help bring these guys down. I'm not alone in this ... and never was.*

Jean gave me an engmatic smile and I honestly don't know if I thought that out loud. Not that I cared. I was beyond tired and it was true. He was one of the good guys, an ally and a friend.

Still, knowing how I felt would go to his head ...

We went to the shore where Others were being rounded up by military personnel. The bombs might not have killed them, but they were still in a heap of trouble.

A soldier handcuffed a robed figure and Jean ran over, stopping him before he could latch on the metal braces. "You don't want to piss off this guy," Jean said to the soldier. "He's the Ferryman. If you jail him, who's going to guide your soul to the beyond?" He turned to the hooded figure and said, "Thank you. I'll get you out and home. Promise."

The figure nodded in thanks.

"Is that the Ferryman—as in Charon?" I said, as Jean hastily guided us to the shoreline and away from the military personnel.

"The one and same," Jean said, waving at a military speedboat that rushed toward the beach. It was manned by the same overenthusiastic kid on the beach. He helped us onto the boat and Jean pushed us out into the water.

"You not jumping in?" I asked.

Jean shook his head. "I'm going to wait for the clean-up crew. And … well, given that the two of you died on the island, it wouldn't be very seemly of me to ride with zombies. Yuk," he said with a smirk. "Besides, me and the boys have some clean up to do. There are monsters on this island and we're going to round up as many as we can."

"Do you need help?" I asked.

Jean grabbed my hand and said, "You've done enough and, besides, if you stick around, you'll be stealing my thunder. Go … go before Shouf figures out you're alive and enlists you. Once I'm back on base, I'll be sure to erase any knowledge of your existence."

And before my brain could stop me, I gave Jean a hug. Pulling away, I cleared my throat and with cheeks I really hoped weren't blushing, said, "I believe the word is 'disavow'. That's what governments do when they forget you."

Jean grinned. "As you wish, Ms. Darling. Consider yourself 'disavowed'. Now go." Jean turned to the kid. "Drop them off away from the base and report back to Kaneda, where you're going to hand them this." He pulled out a piece of paper from his pocket and gave it to the young soldier.

Then turning to me, he said, "Release orders for your friends. Oh, and you'll need this." He handed me my passport. "I suggest that you all meet up at the airport and get the hell out of Dodge City. They won't be looking for you two, not after my report, but I can't shield you from an accidental meeting. And General Shouf does like to wander the streets of Okinawa at night."

I looked at the papers and my passport in my hand. So I was free from indentured, military servitude. "Thank you."

"Don't thank me, ma'am," he said in an exaggerated southern drawl. "Just playing the white knight to your damsel in distress."

"Humph. Still not funny," I said as the young soldier kicked the engine on and sped us onto the waters.

↔

I disobeyed Jean's orders to get the hell out of Dodge for one small and necessary detour.

"You're sure she'll want to see me?" I said to Keiko, but I stared out the car's window into downtown Naha.

"For the third time, I am sure," Keiko said. When we weren't being chased by nio and shisa, she actually didn't drive that fast. But it was still obvious from the way she navigated the streets that she was the most capable driver I'd ever been in a car with, and she knew exactly where she was going. "She sometimes talks about you."

I stared at Keiko. "She does?"

"Yes, especially when I was young. She would tell me the story of the woman who saved her as a little girl during the war."

My eyes filled with tears. In her story, Blue referred to me as "a woman"—not a vampire, not a yokai, but what I had originally been before: just a human like her. I was silent; I didn't know what to say. "She almost died under my care …" I began.

Keiko's hand slid over mine as she pulled us onto a side street and into a small parking lot. When she had put the car in park, she turned to me. "But she didn't—she lived. And because of good people like you and Kenji, my grandmother went on to become a noro."

"Keiko, I …"

"Go see her, Katto-san, before it is too late. My grandmother never misses her afternoon nap."

I smiled through tears and kissed Keiko on the cheek before I stepped out.

↔

Standing at the modest apartment door, my hands trembled as I knocked.

An elderly woman opened the door, her cataract-filled eyes looking up at me before they glazed over with tears of surprise and joy. *"Honto ni, anata da?"*

I nodded. "Yeah, Blue. It's me."

I spent the afternoon with the elderly woman I had saved when she was a child so many years ago. It was the only good thing I ever did as a vampire, and seeing her apartment walls covered with pictures of her daughters, her husband, her grandchildren—pictures of her as a younger woman, travelling to Paris, Rome, the Grand Canyon, Edinburgh—pictures that documented a long, happy life filled with all the moments that mattered—I had never felt prouder.

Blue shuffled forward onto her chair and bowed, her old body crinkling, but I could see her determination; she wasn't going to stop until she managed to honor me.

"No," I said, bowing before kneeling at her feet. "It is I who needs to thank you. You reminded me what it was to be human, and for that, I will forever be in your debt."

↔

Afterward, Keiko drove me to the airport in silence.

Just before we arrived at departures, I said, "Bet you're happy to have me out of your hair."

Keiko laughed. "Yes and no. Despite everything, I see why my grandmother trusted you."

I smiled. "I meant to tell you this before, Keiko: you're just like her. You have the same spirit."

As we pulled up to the curb, Keiko idled the car and bowed to me in her seat. "That is kind of you to say, Kat-sama."

I returned the gesture. "Friends?" I asked.

She gave me a curious look.

"Are we friends? Like can I call you up sometimes and ask you how it's going? See how things are on the island? And with Blue?"

Keiko laughed. "Yes. Friends." She glanced through the window past me. "I think I recognize those faces."

I turned. Deirdre and Egya stood outside departures, nervously waiting for me. They held tickets in their hands.

When I got out, Deirdre nearly lifted me off the ground when she wrapped her arms around me. "Milady," she breathed, "you are unhurt."

"Not first class," Egya lamented as he hugged me afterward. "What the hell happened?"

"We have hours on the plane—I'll tell you everything then. Now, let's get the hell out of here."

We walked into the airport and through customs without incident. The whole time, my soul-filled heart raced with fear that someone would stop us and that I'd be right back to where I was when this all began.

But once we were in line for security, I figured we were in the clear. After all, I literally had nothing on me except a small porcelain jar hanging around my neck. The Soul Jar was so innocuous that I doubted Others would know I held something of immense magical significance, let alone airport security.

The funny thing about fear: what you are afraid of rarely happens. What does happen is something else. Something far, far worse.

At security, I was pulled aside and into a room to be "questioned." I expected to see General Shouf sitting there with her eyeless face staring at me, but there was no aigamuchab. There was no Other there at all. Instead, I was seated across from a middle-aged man of European origin.

The guard who had escorted me in bowed and left the room.

"What's this about?" I asked.

The man ignored me at first, before rasping, "It seems, Katrina Darling, that you've found your soul and lost mine."

(Not) The End

KAT'S ADVENTURES CONTINUE IN RUN, KAT, RUN - OUT SOON!

A BRIEF, SECONDARY EPILOGUE

The Devil has been living on this island almost since the beginning. Well, the beginning of the end. He came to Kakusareta Taiyo Shima not long after the gods left, seeking to contemplate the situation he was in.

After all, his pride had been greatly damaged by their departure, for the gods left without him. How dare they? He was the Devil, Lucifer, the Morning Star, the Adversary, the Angel of the Bottomless Pit. His actions influenced the creation of this world in more impactful ways than the gods themselves. No other creature has had the impact he has had, but despite that, they left him behind.

How dare they?

And so the Devil sits in seclusion, contemplating his new lot in life —his new, *mortal* lot.

Most of his thoughts are preoccupied with anger at the insult thrust upon him. If he could only face the gods, he would tell them exactly what he thinks of their little "creation" experiment. He would berate those gods for abandoning them.

Us.

That's where his thoughts always end. At that one word: *us.* How could they abandon *us*? How could they leave *us* behind? How could they condemn *us* to the slow death of mortality?

The Devil doesn't know what hurts more: their departure or the sad fact that he is no longer the Devil in anything other than name. Now he is an Other, just like the rest of them.

↔

The Devil is sitting in his hut when all the hubbub begins. It starts with human soldiers that insist he evacuate. The soldiers are forceful with the human priestesses and some of the Others on this island. They try to be forceful with him, but the mere sight of him gives the human soldiers pause, their tone no longer forceful, but rather that of fearful children begging forgiveness and offering any and all concessions their limited powers can grant.

It's good to know that the sight of him still inspires fear in the humans. The Devil does not want to die, and agrees to leave the island. But he wishes to be the last to board the departing ferry. He requests, in the way that all his requests are in fact demands, that the soldiers fetch him at the last possible moment, and not a second before.

Then he returns to his hut and continues his contemplations.

In the adjacent hut resides Father Time, the batty old kook. Of all the creatures in existence, Father Time should have known the gods would leave. Hell, he probably did, not that you can get the old bastard to say anything coherent. He is a being that literally lives in all times at once and such existence drives one mad, even for a preternatural creature such as he.

Three humans arrive at Father Time's hut, requesting his help. They speak of the rising gods. *Humph*, the Devil thinks, *you can hardly call Quetzalcoatl, Baldr and Izanami gods*. They are weak, barely-deities who died early in the world's history. They are pathetic, inconsequential gods … who will rise to power if they are not stopped.

The Devil cannot have that, nor can he get directly involved. There are rules, and one rule is his neutrality in such matters. So the Devil does what he always does: he influences from the shadows.

He whispers in the ears of the humans, giving them thoughts they believe to be their own, but are really his. He gives them a hint that, if properly utilized, will help them stop the gods.

Will it work? At this moment it is hard to tell, for the Devil cannot see the future. But if these humans have a chance to stop these gods from rising, it will be because of his help, for a human does not understand how the celestial game is played.

By simply whispering to the one called Kat, "How does Father Time know what will happen to an event that has yet to happen?" the Devil may have very well saved the world.

↔

The Devil finds himself in a slum called Paradise Lot. Clever name. Not such a clever place, though. He has overseen torture chambers prettier than this place. Still, it is his home now, and now that the world will continue on, he must get used to it.

"The world will go on," he muses.

It seems that his tip has indeed saved the world, for the three humans have prevailed, stopping the dead gods from rising.

It is an odd sensation, saving the world. He feels a sense of pride, but that is to be expected—he is the Devil, after all. What is strange is the adjacent sense of joy that mixes in with the pride. He feels ... good for having done something *good*.

And that is when an undeniable thought strikes him like lightning from Michael's sword: in this GoneGod World, the Devil does not need to be evil.

He can be something else here. Something different.

Something better.

And in being something better, he can save the world.

This thought pleases him very much.

But still, saving the world is a Herculean task, and he is but one Other. He will need help—allies—to achieve his goal.

The Devil's lips curl in thoughtful pleasure as he considers who he will approach first. The male human, Jean—a human whose ear he *also* whispered in, telling him another secret that, in time, could *end* the world—spoke of his wife, and how she would do anything to save the world.

He also spoke of how he would do anything in his power to save his Bella. Such devotion. Such *love*.

And if the Devil knows anything, he knows exactly how *love* can be used.

Twisted.

Realigned ...

All in the name of good, of course.

ALSO BY RAMY VANCE

Mortality Bites Series

Mortality Bites

Family Matters

Superhero Me!

Orphaned Follies

Dawn of a Thousand Sunsets

Three Dead Gods

Run, Kat, Run

Encantado Dreams

The Heaviest of Burdens

Looking for a great deal? Grab these book bundles...

Setting Fires with Dragons - complete series

Mortality Bound - complete series

GoneGod World - Complete series

Series Starter - Bundle

ALSO BY RAMY VANCE

Mortality Bites Series

Mortality Bites

Family Matters

Superhero Me!

Orphaned Follies

Dawn of a Thousand Sunsets

Three Dead Gods

Run, Kat, Run

Encantado Dreams

The Heaviest of Burdens

Shattered Vows

GoneGod World Series

GoneGod World

Keep Evolving

CrystalDreams

Penemue's Inferno

Looking for a great deal? Grab these book bundles...

Setting Fires with Dragons - complete series

Mortality Bites - complete series

Mortality Bound - Complete series

Series Starter - Bundle

7

www.ingramcontent.com/pod-product-compliance
Lightning Source LLC
Chambersburg PA
CBHW022008050726
47499CB00003BA/828